THE
COUNTESS
& THE
RAKE

by

GEORGETTE BROWN

THE
COUNTESS
& THE
RAKE

CHAPTER ONE

"WHO *IS* SHE?" marveled Phineas Barclay, adjusting the silken mask he wore to better view the masked woman overlooking a couple in the throes of pleasure. He wished Penelope, the proprietress of *Madame Botreaux's Ballroom of Pleasures*, would add more lighting to the dim underground assembly hall where men and women gathered to indulge their prurient appetites. While he understood the darkness helped to conceal the identity of the patrons, it hindered one's ability to fully admire the form of one's partner—or partners.

"Lady Athena," supplied Lance Duport. A longtime patron and friend of Penelope Botreaux, Lance had ceased to wear a mask many years ago. He eyed Phineas through a quizzing glass. "My dear fellow, that is a bang-up cravat. Do you think your valet could teach mine?"

Phineas smiled. "You have changed little in the years, Duport."

"As have *you*," Lance responded.

Phineas leaned over the rail of the balcony to observe the patrons who had gathered on the ballroom floor below to witness 'Lady Athena' and the handsome man and modish woman pleasuring each other under her watchful gaze. Though she did not possess the sloping shoulders or slender arms admired by most, she was nonetheless a captivating figure—and for reasons beyond her strange costuming. Black leather boots, of the kind worn by men in the military but for the curvaceous Louis heels, encased her legs well past her knees. Her thin chemise fell over swelling hips, and Phineas believed that if a candle were held to it, the material would prove sheer enough to reveal her full and supple thighs. Her corset, an unusual black damask with gold floral embroidery, was loosely laced in the front, revealing the paleness of her breasts, two swollen mounds with nipples peering over the edge of the chemise. Phineas felt a tug at his crotch as he drank in the scintillating curves of her body.

"How droll it is to have you back from your exile, Lord Barclay," commented Penelope, whose rounded figure gave evidence of her affinity for one too many glasses of port.

"Barclay is sufficient," Phineas replied, feeling his jaw tighten as he recalled the five years he had spent on the continent. Devil take it, he had never thought he would miss Yorkshire pudding, but he had. "My brother is his lordship."

"Not with your return. The barony was granted to him only because you were thought dead."

"When you first walked in," Lance added, "I thought I looked upon a bloody ghost."

"Indeed, as you are most certainly not dead, whose body, then, is interred at the Barclay crypt bearing your name?"

"I haven't the foggiest," Phineas replied. "I went into hiding after two attempts were made on my life. I had no notion that the *Comte Le Sur* had proclaimed me dead—with feigned proof."

"Which of his daughters had you seduced?" Lance asked.

"Both."

Penelope waved a dismissive hand. "It matters not. It is more than wonderful to have you alive and returned. I have not had much in the way of an Adonis to feast my eyes upon—not since Vale. Alas, he has not graced our company for nigh on two years." She sighed wistfully. "He used to stand right where you are."

"The Marquess of Dunnesford?" Phineas inquired, turning around to face Penelope. "What induced him to take his leave?"

"He fell in love," Lance answered with a sigh to match Penelope's.

"Dunnesford? In love?" Phineas repeated, incredulous.

Penelope and Lance both nodded. "With his wife."

"The deuce." Phineas shook his head, wondering what other surprises lay in store with his return to England. He turned his attention back to Lady Athena, who carried a crop as if she were the headmaster of a school for truculent boys.

"Does this Lady Athena do naught but watch?" he asked Penelope.

Penelope aimed her quizzing glass at the woman in question, then brought it back towards Phineas, her preferred subject.

"She is my assistant," she replied. "I have delegated most of my duties to her, but she is not the sort to intrigue your attentions "

"All manner of women intrigue me," Phineas responded with a rakish grin.

"You are incorrigible," Lance commented with a shake of his head. "Was it not your entanglement with a woman that forced you from England in the first place?"

Phineas remained quiet. He had no desire to revisit the past. Nor did he know or trust Duport well enough to divulge the entire truth of the affair.

"What does it matter?" Penelope admonished. "From what I heard the duel was more than fair. That Jonathan Weston was killed…"

Phineas turned around to see Penelope clearly wishing she could have swallowed her words. He crossed his arms over his chest. "Who is this Lady Athena?"

She shook her head quickly. "I do not name the identity of my patrons, and Lady Athena has never indicated a desire to reveal herself."

Lance added, "She is one that even you, my friend, will find difficult to conquer."

Phineas raised his brows. "My reputation as a lover must have diminished greatly in my absence."

"Your skills in that vein are of no use with her. She rarely chooses a partner for herself, though there will be a Presenting for new members shortly. In the twelvemonth she has been here, she has selected a man for herself no more than thrice, and allows no one to bring her to climax."

"Odds fish." Phineas had never heard of such a thing. What was the purpose of coming to Madame Botreaux's if one could not attain that sublime euphoria? This Lady Athena was the most peculiar woman. He looked over the balcony to see Lady Athena circling the couple. Was it the boots that lent her stalking such an erotic quality?

"I can see your thoughts, Lord Barclay," Penelope said with a small grin. "I will lay you a wager that what you contemplate cannot be done."

Phineas unloosened his cravat with slow deliberation.

"Alas, a work of art gone in a moment," Lance murmured, but his dismay was easily replaced with a new interest as Phineas began to untie his shirt.

Both Penelope and Lance nearly drooled as the shirt was pulled overhead to reveal a chiseled chest.

"My—my word," Lance stammered. "Have you taken up pugilism?"

"I have. I also spent a good deal of my time on the Continent in Italy, perfecting the art of the sword. Your stakes, madam?" Phineas asked.

"*You*," Penelope pronounced. "I wish you to be mine for a night."

"And if I can seduce the Lady Athena, what is my prize?"

Penelope smiled, envisioning her win already. "Name your price."

"Her name," Phineas answered. "I want to know who she really is."

Penelope glanced down in consideration, but after a brief hesitation, she lifted her chin. "I have witnessed Lady Athena for a year now. As delectable as you are, Barclay, she will not change her ways."

"You wound my pride, madam," Phineas replied, covering his heart in mock pain.

"If she selects you, you will have such time until she casts you aside." Penelope sidled up to him and tapped his chest with her quizzing glass. "At which time, you shall be mine, dear Barclay."

He captured her hand and brought it to his lips. "I adore a wager that knows no loss for me."

Penelope trembled at his touch and had to take a step away from him to breathe.

Phineas bowed.

He turned his attention back to Lady Athena. No woman had yet proven impervious to his charms. His conquests reflected all manner of women from a shy rector's daughter to a frosty matron who disapproved at first of his attentions upon her daughter, then became increasingly envious of her own progeny. Lady Athena possessed the one quality he needed: she was a woman.

Invigorated by the impending challenge, he descended the balcony and prepared himself for the Presenting.

* * * * *

Gertrude "Gertie" Farrington appraised the men and women in the Presenting, a ritual in which new guests and those wishing for a new lover presented themselves for selection. She felt formidable in her new garments. Of particular pride were the boots she had designed herself. The mask she wore was cut from the same fabric as her corset. When first she had donned the name and character of Lady Athena a year ago, she had favored a gold mask. Now black was her preferred color.

Her favorite crop, a symbol of her authority, rested atop her shoulder at a smart angle as she strode down the line with the air of a general inspecting his troops. Senior patrons selected first, but many of them deferred their position to Lady Athena. Out of pity or respect, Gertie knew not. Nor did she care.

She eyed a slender young man of fine form. He had thick lips, and she imagined what it would be like to kiss him. But it had been some time since she had last chosen a patron for herself. She wondered that she would know what to do.

And then her gaze met a pair of intense eyes behind a silver mask. In the dim lighting, she could not discern the color of the eyes, which seemed to capture what little light existed and reflected it back twofold. They stared at her with unnerving intensity. Feeling as if she might drown in their pools, she pulled her gaze wider and contemplated the whole of the physiognomy. Though his mask covered half his face, the shadows suggested a striking appearance.

The body, too, was beautiful. He stood a head taller than she, and had a pleasing proportion, neither wide and brawny nor long and lanky. She imagined running her hands over the ridges of his chest and caressing his strapping thighs. His muscles, sleek but not burly, exposed an aristocratic background full of sport. His calves were well defined, as was the bulge in his breeches.

Conscious that he was still staring at her with unabashed impudence, she raised her brows at him. She had never seen him before, though she could not be certain as most of the patrons hid their identity behind masks. He did not seem to understand the position of authority she held here or he would have assumed a more deferential air.

Strange, but he seemed to read her thoughts in the way that he looked at her. For the first time since becoming a regular at Madam Botreaux's, she felt herself faltering. Her heart seemed to palpitate unevenly. Walking past him, she spotted a more callow fellow who puffed his chest forward in a display of undue confidence. Just as she was about to pass on selecting anyone for the evening, she heard a voice behind her. His voice *felt like velvet*, if such a thing were possible, its resonation low and comforting.

"Afraid, my lady?"

Gertie could feel the blood pounding a warning in her ears. She turned slowly towards the man with the bright eyes. "It is customary that those in the Presenting line not speak lest spoken to."

"Am I to be punished for it?"

His response startled and puzzled her.

"It would seem you are new here," she replied, trying not to appear nettled. "As such, your transgression may be forgiven."

"Are you afraid to administer the punishment?"

She stared at him in disbelief. Had he twice called her afraid? Rising to his challenge, she responded, "Consider yourself spared."

"That fails to answer my query."

She sucked in her breath, then enunciated the difference. "Not afraid. I am *disinclined.*"

The corner of his mouth curled. "Ah. Of course."

Of course? What the devil did he mean by that? Did he presume to know her better than herself? Realizing her vexation growing, she took a deep breath and eyed him more keenly. Who was this stranger and why these attempts to insult her?

"Is it punishment you be wanting?" she asked him imperially.

At last he displayed deference by bowing his head. He said in a low baritone, "If you would give it, my lady."

She shivered for it felt as if his words had caressed her skin. No man in recent memory had provoked her with such efficacy. She straightened in triumph, but he dashed the cup of victory as quickly from her lips.

"And if you dare," he added. When he looked up, there was a glimmer in his eyes.

If she selected him, then his stratagem prevailed. If she did not, she risked validating his accusations. The great Lady Athena feared no one—even if this man, with his uncanny ability to unsettle her, possessed an air of danger.

Her pride carried the day.

She put the tip of her crop upon his pectoral. He did not flinch.

"You will rue your words," she informed him. "Towards that end, I would be much *inclined.*"

He bowed his head in acknowledgement. "I am yours, my lady. At your disposal and your command."

The words rang heady promise, but she tried to ignore their echoes. She stalked towards one of the many arched alcoves that lined the main assembly hall. The stranger followed behind her.

Located at the far end of the ballroom, her alcove looked upon the length of the assembly hall. On the opposite end wound the large staircase that led to the balcony of Madame Botreaux. She had once been invited to join Penelope on the balcony but had declined. She preferred proximity to the patrons, which allowed her to catch every gasp, every furrow of the brown, every moan of pleasure—all experiences that she might never know for herself.

The furnishing in the alcove consisted of a table, chair and wide chaise. The dim lighting came from a lone candelabra. Gertie indicated the stranger should stand in the center. To her relief, he did as she directed without word. She took a deep breath and began to circle him. She knew not what to make of him. He had successfully provoked her into selecting him, inviting her to punish him of all things. Perhaps she would. His behavior certainly merited a set-down.

"What brings you here?" she asked at last.

"I presume the same *raison d'être* that brings you here," he replied without wavering his gaze. "Lady Athena."

The smoothness of his voice made her shiver, but the tone irked her. She sensed a veiled taunt.

"Who are you?"

"I would trade my identity only for yours," he answered.

"Then I shall call you Hephaestus whilst you are mine," she

pronounced with a deliberate smirk for Hephaestus was a lame and therefore grotesque god in Greek mythology, but he only smiled as if he shared in her mirth.

Walking behind him, she eyed the curve of his rump—round, hard and smooth beneath his tight breeches.

"Is my lady pleased by what meets her eye?"

*The devil...*Gertie stared at him in disbelief. Who was this man and how did he seem to know her thoughts?

"You are forward," she informed him.

"I prefer it to pretenses."

Did he mean to accuse her again? She began to relish the opportunity to lord over him. For the night only. She had never committed herself to any man for considerable length of time—save for the one that she was bound to by law and vow—her husband, the Earl of Lowry. The reason for her patronage at Madame Botreaux's. The stranger before her had presumed that they possessed some shared interest in coming to the *Ballroom*, but he knew nothing of her situation.

"Modesty and manners are not the same as pretenses," she said.

"And what purpose do your modesty and manners serve? I find them rather strangely placed in an establishment such as this."

Once more she was taken aback by his audacity.

"By the quality of your speech, one might presume you to have been born into breeding," she said, "but you display a great lack of it, sir."

"Hephaestus," he reminded her.

She felt the color rise in her cheeks.

"I freely own that my governess had more than one occasion to reprimand me," he said. "I give you leave to do the same if you are so inclined and if your modesty and manners would allow it."

"I am inclined!" she snapped before she could think of aught else to say.

"Then shall we commence? What manner of punishment would you like to administer?"

She was at a loss. She had never punished anyone before, but Lady Athena would have no qualms. She would make Hephaestus rue his impudence.

"The headmaster at my school for boys would—" he began.

"Yes, I think that a fitting place to start."

Her response surprised him for a change.

"Brace yourself against my writing table," she directed.

As he did so, she felt herself growing warm, an uncommon occurrence. In her time at Madame Botreaux's, she had observed many an arse, perhaps few as beguiling as his or accented so well by such tight fitting breeches, but certainly enough agreeable ones. Why did this one call to her, tugging at some primal urge embedded deep within her body?

"Let fall your breeches," she commanded. A tremble went through her.

He did as instructed without the least bit of timidity.

Dear bodkins. She stared at the molded buttocks. Naked, his arse was even more inspiring. Shaking her head, she forced herself to concentrate on the task at hand. She was Lady Athena, about to discipline an unruly boy.

Taking a deep breath, she backhanded one arse cheek with the crop. He did not flinch. She landed another on the other cheek. Still no movement from him.

"My lady, those blows are mere tickles compared to what I have endured as a boy," he said.

Gathering her strength, she dealt him three successive whacks in the same spot. This time she heard a small grunt. Even in the dim lighting, she could see the faint mark of where the crop had struck. She wanted to reach out and touch him there, caress his arse, perhaps even plant a kiss.

"Better," he complimented. "But still fairly weak."

Swallowing a growl of frustration, she struck him again, and again, and again, hoping the rhythm would diffuse the strange effect she was experiencing. But the vigorous spanking did not excise her disconcertion. On the contrary, she felt more flustered. Although he seemed to grip the table more tightly, he displayed little evidence of the sensations he must be feeling. The only one who seemed to be out of sorts was her. She was breathing hard from her exertion, and the sight of his body taking all she gave had only caused her to flush more intensely.

Not knowing quite how to proceed next, she adjusted her mask and told him to don his breeches. "We are done. For tonight."

The words were out her mouth before she had proper time to consider what she said. Though she had thought to be done with him, she was curious to see if he would return chastened. After buttoning the breeches, he stood erect, his posture emphasizing his broad shoulders.

"Thank you, Lady Athena."

She nodded even though he faced away from her. The ensuing silence made her agitate her crop against her thigh. She let out a deep breath. "You will return two nights hence to this space. If I do not find you here waiting for me by ten o'clock, I am done with you."

He turned around to give her a bow. "I am your servant, Lady Athena, and will do all that you bid."

She strode out, not daring to glance back. She hoped he would not return.

CHAPTER TWO

THE STRIDENT VOICE of Dowager Lowry transcended the stairs as if she meant to call to someone on the second floor instead of speaking to her son in the drawing room where she waited. "I do hope your wife has not selected that dreadful gown of peach for the Bennington ball. Peach is not a becoming color upon her."

Standing alone at the top of the stairs, Gertie glanced down upon the gown of peach she wore. With her dark brown curls and pale complexion, she had thought the pastel an appropriate color for herself. The satin gown with its layered lace ruffles at the elbows was one of her favorites to start the Season. She wore it with matching slippers and had labored to find the best among her jewelry to accent her attire, finally settling on her garnet set. Despite her impatience, she had allowed the coiffeuse to produce curl after curl in a meticulous attempt to create the *Merveilleuse*. For a brief moment, Gertie considered donning another gown, but they were late for the Bennington ball as it was, and she had the suspicion that the most perfect gown would not meet the approval of the Dowager.

"Or that horrid gown of lavender she wore to the Wempole garden party," Sarah Farrington, her sister-in-law, added.

"Then why do you not impart your sensibilities to her?" Gertie heard her husband retort with irritation. "Instead you allow me to appear at these events with an unflattering wife."

"I protest. I have made such an attempt, but alas, it has proven futile."

Gertie recalled Sarah's one endeavor. Her sister-in-law had reviewed her wardrobe, sniffing at the mediocrity of certain articles and explaining how each gown was unsuited for a woman of her shape and features before declaring the whole effort to be quite fatiguing and that surely it was time for tea? Gertie would have gladly taken any guidance from her sister-in-law for Sarah was a beauty of the first order and followed all the latest fashion plates in *The Lady's Magazine.*

"Her arms appear to have grown in thickness," Dowager Lowry disapproved. "I hope you have cautioned her, Alexander, against indulging her appetite too much."

Weary of overhearing more criticisms from her in-laws, Gertie made her entrance into the drawing room. Three pairs of eyes looked her over from head to toe. Alexander and his mother frowned while Sarah smirked upon seeing the gown of peach. Gertie was well aware that she was the ugly duckling among the statuesque Farringtons. Though she knew the Earl to have born more affection for her dowry than her person, she had considered herself fortunate to have acquired a husband who had such fine features. With only a modest countenance and a plump figure, Gertie had been convinced she could only marry a skinny freckled young man or a corpulent wizened man with a gout ailment. Alexander with his golden locks, fair skin, and high cheekbones had appeared a dashing prince.

They had been married three years. The fairy tale had withered soon after their wedding.

Alexander narrowed his eyes at the gown of offense. "Shall we increase your allowance, Gertie, that you may procure a suitable ball gown?"

He asked for the benefit of his mother for he knew the answer. Alexander had squandered the largesse of the dowry and inheritance, most of it upon procuring a new coach-and-four and a house in Berkeley Square—though he considered Grosvenor Square a more fitting address for an Earl—and the remainder at dice, horses, and pugilism. His flippancy with all matters monetary had led his steward to begin consulting with his wife, whom they discovered had a decent head for figures and possessed more common sense. His distaste for such responsibilities trumped his pride, and Alexander was content to have his wife oversee the handling of the estate and household economy, provided he had access to funds when he needed them.

"Perhaps we ought to consider a new dressing maid," Sarah

added, raising two perfectly arched brows in her continued inspection of Gertie. "Jane has not done a proper job of disguising the shadows beneath your eyes."

During the first year of her marriage to Alexander, the criticisms from her sister-in-law came in the form of poorly conceived flattery—a la "the bonnet you wear today is much more flattering than the one you wore yesterday." Sarah made no effort nowadays to temper her contempt. Gertie allowed that such a beauty as Sarah must easily find fault in lesser mortals and had once quipped to a friend that Sarah should be glad that her splendor shined all the more when standing beside her plain sister-in-law. The angels had blessed Sarah Farrington with locks made from the sun's rays, a swan-like neck, dainty feet and wrists so slender they equaled those of a child. Her nose, like her mother's, was perhaps too sharp in profile, but apart from that, she was flawless.

"Perhaps a little more powder then?" Gertie replied, attempting to view herself in a mirror on the opposite wall.

"We have delayed long enough," Alexander said with impatience.

Sarah had exceptionally discerning eyes, Gertie reassured herself as the Farringtons stepped into their carriage. Jane had received specific instructions to blend away the shadows—the result of an unfortunate series of events from the night before. Even now Gertie felt a warm discomfort as she recalled *him*. Hephaestus she had dubbed him, but the name had done little to achieve what she had hoped. Never had a visit to *Madame Botreaux's* proven so unsatisfactory. She had been in fine form until he had appeared.

The night had progressed from bad to worse when, upon arriving to Lowry House last night, she had discovered that the portico she kept ajar for her surreptitious return had been shuttered. She had stood outside in the dark of night for what seemed like hours contemplating her options. She could knock on the door and wake the servants, perhaps explaining that she had gone for a walk to quiet a restless night, but that would not clarify how the door came to be locked after her. She finally remembered that she had left the window of her bed chamber ajar. She had successfully climbed the vines to reach the balcony of her chambers, but only after scraping a knee and losing a slipper to the bushes below.

"The Henshaws announced the birth of child—a boy," remarked Dowager Lowry as their carriage veered onto Bourdon Street. "The Duchess had been rather apprehensive that Elizabeth would not produce an heir, but I had assured her that her daughter would fulfill her responsibility."

Gertie stared into her hands. She felt the pointed gaze of the Dowager. The Dowager never failed to announce a birth of note—one would have thought her the bloody *Times*—to underscore the fact that she had no grandchild. Gertie felt Alexander shift beside her. She had once told her mother-in-law, despite the delicacy of the matter, that it was not for want of trying. In truth, as much as she dreaded the conjugal act with her husband, she would have liked nothing more than to cradle a babe of her own. Alexander, however, seemed to have lost interest in the past twelvemonth. He had not touched her in some time.

"Gertie, have you been seeing Dr. Fitzwilliam?" the Dowager inquired. "He told me you have not scheduled an appointment with him in over three months. I took the liberty of inviting him over next Tuesday. You will make the engagement at one o'clock, I presume?"

Gertie glanced at Alexander, but he directed his gaze out the window. There would be no help from him on this matter.

"I wonder that his services are needed—or effective?" Gertie returned.

The nostrils of the Dowager flared. "Do you doubt his skill, Gertie? Elizabeth Henshaw was a patient of his."

With an inward sigh, Gertie relented.

Sarah arranged her skirts of midnight blue about her with long slender fingers. "I suppose the benefit of our supreme tardiness is that we are likely to pull straight up to the house, but then we will have missed much of the amusement, and the embarrassment of it all is most difficult to bear. I wonder that any other woman has to endure sharing a dressmaid with *two* other women? Shall we be forever late to all our events?"

She pinned her accusatory stare at Gertie, who was tempted to respond that most women had not the luxury of a dressing maid at all, but instead she replied, "I think that no one save ourselves shall be cognizant of why we are late."

"It is enough that I am aware!" Sarah snapped.

Gertie looked to her husband, though she knew that he would not defend her or offer that he had acquiesced to her suggestion that they reign in their expenses by releasing some of the servants. She suspected that he had easily agreed in part because dismissing the other maids would have had little impact upon his person. Alexander had been more reluctant to dismiss the groomsman, but when Gertie explained that they had exhausted their credit and that the only possible loan would have to come from Jewish quarters, he had conceded.

Silence pervaded most of the ride to the Bennington residence. Alexander spent the time examining his fingernails, Sarah pouted, and the Dowager stared at Gertie, who had long ceased to attempt a light tete-a-tete with her family. Inevitably, they would find something at fault with her. As Sarah predicted, there was no line of carriages to wait behind when they arrived, and when they were announced, most of the guests were too engrossed in conversation already to notice. Sarah was not often of a cheerful disposition, but Gertie braced herself for what would surely be at least a sennight worth of her cantanker.

Gertie anticipated a long night as her best friend, the Marchioness of Dunnesford, would not be in attendance. The dancing had already begun. Not expecting to dance—Alexander had yet to request a single dance since their marriage—Gertie went to sit beside Mrs. Pemberly, a woman who had befriended her parents before they had passed away.

"Gertrude, how lovely to see you," Mrs. Pemberly greeted with a warm smile that extended to her emerald eyes, which had lost none of their radiance through the years. She patted the spot on the settee next to her. "Ah, you wore that dress last Season, did you not? It is a lovely gown, but I must confess that I think the shade to be less than brilliant against your hue, my dear."

"That would seem to be the prevailing sentiment then," Gertie sighed as she took a seat and watched as a flock of men circled around Sarah for the minuet.

"Indeed?"

"My mother-in-law and Sarah commented upon the same."

"That won't do. I have no wish to be in accordance with Belinda Farrington."

Gertie smiled. Mrs. Pemberly had never been enamored of the Farringtons and had cautioned her father against the Earl of Lowry. It was Gertie herself—or her vanity, rather—and the desire of her father to see his only child married that had sanctioned the match.

"There he stands—across the room," Mrs. Drake, sitting on the other side of Mrs. Pemberly, whispered behind her fan.

Mrs. Pemberly promptly held up her own fan. "The one in white silk? With the gold embroidery?"

"Need you ask?"

One corner of Mrs. Pemberly's mouth curled in almost *naughty* fashion, to Gertie's great surprise. Intrigued by the mystery of their exchange, Gertie looked across the ballroom and immediately discerned what had to be the subject of their attention.

Wearing a magnificent coat that curved away from the front to reveal a gorgeous waistcoat and *very* fitting breeches, he was easily the most beautifully dressed man in attendance. The coat had a standing collar trimmed with embroidery, buttoned pleats, and encased his body with such tightness one wondered how he had fit into it. A deep sapphire of the brilliant cut was nestled in his cravat. He wore his hair powdered, smooth about the forehead with *ailes de pigeon* above the ear. Gertie had never seen the man before. Although his high fashion might have escaped her notice, his features would not. With an intelligent brow, a masterful but not overly square jaw, a straight nose, smooth cheeks, and defined lips, he possessed the perfect blend of fair and rugged beauty. His relaxed eyelids gave him a sense of *ennui*. If he was cognizant that he was the center of much attention, he did not reveal it.

Gertie strained to see the color of his eyes until she realized he was looking at her. She jerked her gaze away. Perhaps he had not been looking at her. He stood across the length of the ballroom and from such a distance it would be impossible to know precisely where he gazed. And why would he choose to be looking at her? Still, it had felt as if he had. Perhaps he meant to return the impertinence of her own stare.

"Who is he?" Gertie asked.

"One who has been on all our tongues the whole of the

evening," Mrs. Drake responded.

"What a delicious thought," Mrs. Pemberly quipped.

Gertie gasped. She had never heard Mrs. Pemberly speak in such a fashion.

"Oh, but you must know him, Gertie. He is a cousin to your husband, is he not?"

Gertie furrowed her brows. "I have not met him before."

Mrs. Pemberly nodded. "Yes. He went into exile, as it were, some five years ago, before you were married to Alexander. And then we all thought him dead at the hands of a French count whose daughter Barclay was rumored to have seduced. But you must know Barclay's sisters and brother. Lord Barclay is the eldest."

Mrs. Drake shook her head. "Lady Surrington is the eldest of the brood."

"The Baron Barclay—I supposed he is no longer the Baron then," Gertie said of the younger brother. "He is not only a cousin to the Earl but a neighbor. The Barclay lands borders Lowry. I had forgotten he had an older brother."

"I understand the Farringtons are not overly fond of the Barclays?"

"They do not converse much," Gertie rephrased. She deliberated whether or not to take a second look at the man and decided against it.

Not to be deterred from her efforts to unearth more gossip, Mrs. Drake asked, "I heard that if there is no heir for Lowry, the earldom would fall to Lord Barclay? Perhaps that is the reason for his return to England?"

"Hush, Pamela!" Mrs. Pemberly interceded. "If Barclay were interested in peerage, why would he have given up his barony to his brother?"

"He could not manage his estate while in exile. And because an earldom awaits him!"

"Pamela, you are a ninny. Have you forgotten his repute? Barclay has shown he has but one overriding interest: the *fair sex*. I wish I were twenty years younger that I should be an object of his pursuit."

"You need not be. I heard he also courted an Italian countess while in exile, and she had fifty years to her!"

"He has kept his habits then?" Gertie asked for she had heard that Barclay had left England after a duel over a man's wife.

"I should hope so," Mrs. Pemberly responded as she fanned herself more vigorously.

Gertie shook her head and smiled. She rose to her feet. "I think I should look for my husband."

"His years on the Continent have served him well," Mrs. Drake said to Mrs. Pemberly.

Unable to resist any more, Gertie glanced in Lord Barclay's direction, but he was gone.

* * * * *

She dashed behind the heavy damask curtain. Hiding in the Bennington library was not the most dignified activity for the Countess of Lowry, but Gertie would not have anyone witness her tears. Crying did not become her. Her cheeks turned red as apples, the tip of her nose likened itself to a cherry and her eyes puffed pink as the flesh of melons until the whole of her face was a veritable fruit cart.

Lord and Lady Bennington were dear friends, and Lady Bennington had been months planning her first ball of the Season. Gertie did not want the hostess thinking that the event was anything less than a complete triumph with all of her guests. That the evening was proving to be the worst that Gertie could remember was no fault of the Benningtons.

She had gone to seek Alexander in the card room upon suspecting that he might take to hazard, his game of choice whenever he felt short of funds. She had requested to speak to him to remind him that, given their situation, he should limit his gaming. Alexander had turned red with rage.

"Do not *ever* presume to call me away from the tables," he had seethed before stalking back into the card room to, more likely than not, run up more debt.

A little shaken by his vehemence, Gertie had returned to the ballroom to Mrs. Pemberly and Mrs. Drake, both of whom were still on the topic of Lord Barclay. After sitting a while, Gertie had grown restless and decided to seek some air in the gardens, but she had not walked far when she overheard two familiar voices.

"I have not the least interest in Mr. Warburton!" Sarah was protesting.

"It matters not," Alexander had responded, "He has an interest in you."

"But he is *old* and—and *homely*."

"He is wealthy."

"I will *not* marry him."

"As your brother, it is my duty to oversee your interests. We are in a precarious way with funds."

"*My* interests? You mean your interests! Perhaps if you did not lavish your mistress with gifts quite so often, we would not be in such dire straits. That sapphire bracelet of hers must have cost a fair guinea."

The rest of their conversation had continued as if from the end of a long tunnel for Gertie. The words had hit her full and hard in the stomach. Alexander had a mistress. She was not surprised by the fact, but the realization was nonetheless painful. Little wonder that he had not sought her bed chambers of late. He had a mistress. A mistress to whom he presented gifts. Aside from his wedding gift to her, a broach that had belonged to his grandmother, she had never received the slightest token from him.

She could not remember if she had stayed to hear the end of their dialogue. Overcome with misery, she had sought seclusion to nurse her wounds. In the quiet of the library, away from the music and merriment, she had sobbed. She had never expected to win her husband's heart, but she had hoped to have a child, a source of pride and joy, someone to bestow the bountiful affection that waited in her own heart. She was sure that a child would take away the despair of her loveless marriage and fill the void with light. But if her husband had no desire…

What a stupid fool I have been, Gertie had chided herself, on the verge of a new wave of tears when she heard a scuffle outside the library door. She dashed behind the nearest curtain.

Two bodies stumbled into the room. Through the slit between the curtains, she saw the flash of a familiar midnight blue as the bodies fell onto the sofa not far from where she hid. Her cheeks flamed when she realized the body of the woman writhing below was that of her sister-in-law. The body pinning Sarah to the sofa was that of Lord Barclay.

"Tell me," Sarah said between deep breaths, "how it is we have not met before?"

"You would feign ignorance?" he responded as he pressed his mouth to her neck. "Come, come, we have been neighbors, after all."

"I had not had my come-out when you left England. I was five and ten, and I think you thought me an awkward little girl then—"

She stopped upon realizing she had revealed her own falsehood. She looked at him with some trepidation, but he only smiled briefly before returning to her neck, which he caressed in slow lingering kisses. She closed her eyes and moaned in delight.

"You have no need to prevaricate with me, Lady Sarah. You were never awkward."

Sarah arched her back and neck, allowing him more surface. "I see that you have lost none of your impudence since leaving England."

"Indeed, I have acquired more during my absence," he murmured into her neck. "I would hazard that you prefer your men impertinent."

Sarah gasped. One of his hands had made its way up her skirts. Gertie flushed. This would not do. She had to find a way out. But she could not tear her eyes from them—from him and what he was doing. There was something masterful in the way he moved with Sarah, plying her body as if he were a puppeteer secure in knowing just how she would react to his every move. No doubt his confidence stemmed from many a practiced seduction.

"Very impertinent," Sarah acquiesced as her gasps quickened.

Gertie marveled at how this Barclay could fondle Sarah with one hand without interrupting the rhythm of his kisses. Imagining what he might be doing beneath Sarah's skirts stirred sensations in her own loins. His ministrations were apparently quite effective for Sarah was panting and moaning, one hand clutching the edge of the sofa with whitening knuckles. Gertie shifted her weight in discomfort. She needed to find a way out for she knew not how long they intended to stay, and though the fullness with which his mouth explored the neck before him mesmerized her, she did not think she wanted to view her sister-in-law much more than she had.

Sarah's moaning became high pitched grunts and wails. She was close to her climax, her eyes shut tight. The two were absorbed enough for Gertie to slip away. Slowly, she brushed aside the curtain and stepped from her hiding place. Her toe struck the footstool as she dashed towards the door, but she suppressed her cry. Once safely outside the library, she hurried down the hallway and allowed herself a grimace for her poor toe. She found a mirror on the wall and examined how her tears had smeared her powder and rouge.

She also noticed one of her earrings to be missing.

* * * * *

Just before Sarah cried out in ecstasy, Phineas thought he heard something behind him. After gently coaxing the last tremors from her orgasm, he allowed her a moment of peace before moving himself to examine the room about them. He saw no one, but the door was not completely shut and he was sure that he had closed it when they came in.

"What is it?" Sarah murmured as she stretched with the satisfaction of a cat freshly woken from a nap.

"Nothing," he responded. There was no need to alarm her. "I think dinner will be served shortly. We had best return."

It was possible someone had sought to enter the library and he had simply not heard the door open. Sarah had been rather vocal. But then he noticed the overturned footstool. Someone had been in the room.

"When shall I see you again?"

"Methinks your brother bears little fondness for me, madam," he answered wryly as he studied a spot of discoloration on the carpet.

Sarah pouted. "What does that matter?"

It was no discoloration. He bent down and picked up a garnet earring.

"Alexander may be my brother, but I am near twenty years of age and quite capable of deciding whose company I wish to keep."

"No doubt, but I have no desire to find myself in another duel."

He tucked the earring into the pocket of his waistcoat.

"Alexander would never have the courage to challenge you."

Phineas had to agree with her assessment. He had seen enough of Alexander, who was near in age to his own brother, growing up to believe that the Earl lacked much of a backbone. But it had been made clear to him that the scandal of another duel would send him into permanent exile or to a trial by peers. A friend of his who served in the House of Lords had advised him not to test his luck with the latter, saying "If you hadn't made half of them a cuckold by bedding their wives, I would have said otherwise."

Turning to Sarah, Phineas offered his hand. She rose from the sofa and straightened her skirts.

"I will be at Hyde Park tomorrow," she informed him as she patted her ringlets to ensure they had not come undone. "I should be most pleased to see you there—if you are not otherwise occupied."

He brought her delicate hand to his lips. "I will make myself *un*occupied."

She gave him a broad smile, one that looked odd upon her customarily humorless physiognomy. It amused him at times the women he chose to seduce. With Sarah Farrington, she was as much the seducer as he. Having made eye contact with him, she had immediately thrust up her fan, but her eyes had told him all he needed to know. They had beckoned, and when he had not immediately responded for he had no desire to be part of the group of pups that lapped at her, she had sought him out, conveniently dropping her fan at his feet when their paths crossed in the hallways.

At dinner, Sarah glanced often over her pigeon pie in his direction. She was not the only one to eye him. He was keenly aware that he and not the much touted lobster was the cynosure of the evening. There was not one pair of eyes that did not look his way. One set in particular had caught his attention. The soft green eyes, set in an unremarkable but tender physiognomy of rounded cheeks and supple lips, had studied him from across the dance floor. He had found her familiar, and though he possessed an astute memory for faces, he could not place her.

"When did the Earl of Lowry marry?" he asked of Mrs. Pemberly, who was seated next to him.

"He has been married to Gertie some three years," she replied, clearly pleased to be the source of information for him.

He looked down the table at the Countess of Lowry. She did not appear to be the kind of wife he would have expected Alexander to take.

"I do not think I know her family."

"Well, her family is of the *bourgeoisie* but a good family nonetheless. Her father made quite the profit in the sugar trade."

Ah, that explained Alexander's choice of spouse, Phineas thought to himself. He had known Alexander to be rather vain and would not otherwise have taken a plain woman to wife lest she possessed some other prevailing quality.

"If you ask me," Mrs. Pemberly posited, "I would rate her family above that of the Farringtons. Gertie is far too good for the likes of him."

He studied the elder woman and decided she spoke sincerely and not with any attempt to flatter him with her awareness that the Farringtons and Barclays were not the fondest of relations. Mrs. Pemberly seemed a woman who hesitated not to speak her mind. He returned his attention to that of the Countess, who stirred her soup aimlessly. She sat between Alexander and the Dowager Lowry, both of whom ignored her the whole of the dinner. Phineas recalled seeing the Earl and his wife earlier in the evening. He stood too far to overhear their conversation, but he had seen the livid expression upon Alexander and the forlorn look of hopelessness in Lady Lowry after he had berated her in what must have been harsh terms. Though he knew not her person, Phineas felt a tug of sympathy for the Countess. He knew of few women he would recommend Alexander to. Perhaps Sarah Farrington if she were not already his sister.

The powder and rouge upon Lady Lowry wanted another application, he noticed. His gaze drifted to her garnet necklace, the design of which matched the earring in his pocket.

"I should introduce myself to this new relation of mine," he commented.

Mrs. Pemberly eyed him carefully. "Indeed?"

"The relations between the Barclays and the Farringtons are not as strained as the rumors would have you believe. We converse quite amicably."

"Indeed?"

He looked her square in the eyes and smiled. "Indeed."

She was the first to blink. "Well, you will find Gertie a pleasant and *honest* girl. She is quite refreshing in that regard. You will find no nonsense with her. While she may not be up to snuff with all the *de rigueur* of gentle society, she is extremely *sensible*. I myself have seen her maturation through the years and regard her with as much affection as if she were mine own."

Noting the claws of the lioness, he replied, "You are protective of her."

"I will not see her harmed."

"And you fear that I am a wolf in search of a sheep."

"Though I suspect Lady Lowry is not the type to inspire your predilections, I confess your motives puzzle me."

"A simple desire to acquaint myself with a new member of the family does not satisfy you?"

"Certainly the marital situation of a woman has not stopped you before," she continued without answering him, cognizant of the rhetorical nature of his question. "Dare I presume that you have mended your ways?"

A brash question deserved a brash reply.

"Do you hope that I have?"

Mrs. Pemberly colored, then allowed a grin to creep into her lips. "Fair enough."

The dinner over, Phineas rose to his feet. He turned to Mrs. Pemberly and raised her hand to his lips. "What delightful dinner company you have been, Mrs. Pemberly. I esteem a woman who speaks her mind. I hope that Fortune will grace me again with your presence."

The blush rose in her cheeks once more. She raised a thin eyebrow at him. "I rather think that your sojourn on the Continent was spent not in repentance but in perfecting your charms, Lord Barclay."

"You are a woman after mine own heart," he noted of her ability to compliment and critique in the same stroke.

She fluttered her fan before her with a little more vigor. He offered her his arm and escorted her from the dining hall. Across the room, Alexander was engrossed in a conversation with another gentleman, leaving his wife alone to walk behind him.

Mrs. Pemberly must have noticed the same for she said, "Did you not wish to make the acquaintance of the Countess of Lowry?"

Phineas bowed to his dinner companion and made his way towards the Countess.

"Lady Lowry," he addressed.

She had begun to walk away from the crowd, perhaps attempting to steal away to some haven of solitude, and was obviously startled that someone had called to her. When she turned to face him, he saw that she was not as plain as when seen from afar. Her cheeks had a natural blush, and though her eyes were not the large sparkles of color that graced the physiognomy of her sister-in-law, they possessed more depth. Unlike the shallow waters of Sarah Farrington, the verdant eyes of the Countess intrigued him.

They stared at him in displeasure.

Undaunted, he introduced himself with a bow. "I am Phineas Barclay, a relation of the Farringtons."

"I am aware that you are a *distant* relation," she replied coolly.

He had the feeling that even though she had to crane her neck to meet his gaze, she was attempting to look down at him. Perhaps she shared the sentiments of her husband towards the Barclays.

"A much belated congratulations on your nuptials."

Her frown deepened. He would have not have been surprised to hear her tell him that congratulations were unnecessary from him as he had not been invited to the wedding.

"Yes," she said, mustering more hauteur into her expression, "I was told you had been banished to France."

Her dislike of him, which was becoming increasingly palpable, amused him, as did most of the disdain people would have towards him. The son of parents who shocked gentle society with their wanton spirit and numerous illicit affairs, he had become immune at a tender age to what others thought.

"You put it harshly, madam. I like to think of my time there as a holiday," he replied. "I had occasion to travel to the *Côte-d'Or* and would highly recommend the region. The wines there are *par excellence.*"

He could tell his impudence riled her.

"Ah, then you will be taking yourself back there?"

He nearly chuckled at her juvenile attempt to rid herself of his company. "I shall be staying in England for some time. I have come across a pursuit of great interest to me."

"Yes, I know," she said wryly.

"You do?"

She faltered, "I mean…naturally you will have missed much of what England has to offer, perhaps not the same quality of wine that you would find in France, but perhaps a rousing game of cricket or warm Yorkshire pudding on a cool winter morning, and certainly friends and family, from whom I will keep you no longer."

She turned to leave. He refrained from specifying that she was now family.

"Before you leave, Lady Lowry," he said, stopping her in her tracks. "I believe this to be yours."

He held out the earring. Her eyes widened upon seeing it. She hesitated, as if she contemplated denying ownership, but it was obvious that her one ear was missing its adornment. When she reached for the earring, he deftly reached for her with his free hand, pulling her closer. Though the nearest guest was not within earshot, he meant his words for her ears alone.

"Next time, feel free to join us, Countess," he murmured as he pressed the earring into her hand.

She burned brightly to the tips of her ears. Grasping the earring, she turned on her heel and hurried away from him.

CHAPTER THREE

"Y OU APPEAR PERTURBED, my dear. Are you well?" asked Penelope Botreaux.

Gertie realized she had been staring into the distance, clenching and unclenching her crop, as she stood at the top of the stairs that descended into the *Ballroom*.

"No—I mean to say yes, I am well, thank you," Gertie hastened to reply.

"That is a remarkable corset. I have never seen the likes of it before."

Penelope held up her quizzing glass to admire the scarlet satin. Gertie had fashioned the corset over a year ago but had never had the bravado to don it till tonight. She wore it over a black chemise, also an unorthodox article of her own making; her customary black boots; and a black satin mask decorated with three slender plumes emerging from its centre.

"Your gentleman awaits you," Penelope informed with an eccentric smile and a tone of…impatience.

Gertie nodded. Though she had hoped he would not return, tonight she felt differently. Tonight she was ready for him. Tonight she was Lady Athena. Strong and powerful. Not the pitiful Lady Lowry who had cried over an undeserving husband and flushed before a presumptuous rake. The mortification she had felt at the Bennington ball after her encounter with Lord Barclay had turned into anger. She had never met such an insolent and despicable person. That he should not be rotting in Fleet for having murdered young Jonathan Weston in that duel was a travesty of justice.

Yes, murdered. In the court of her opinion, she had tried and found him guilty. No matter that the seconds, his and that of Weston, all refused to elaborate on what had occurred, as if they had taken a vow of silence. Rumors had it that Weston, having been made a cuckold by Barclay, had challenged the latter. That Barclay had been tumbling Mrs. Weston was apparently common knowledge.

Gertie shuddered. And now he had chosen Sarah Farrington for a lover. His choice of Sarah convicted him as much as anything. Gertie could think of no one more vile than Phineas Barclay, and when she recalled how roused she had been in the Bennington library, she despised him more. She had already heard his parents to have been quite the wantons. His older sister, now a widowed Duchess, had a string of lovers that might have rivaled her brother's in number. His second sister was currently engaged in a scandalous *crim con*. The youngest sister had not had her come-out, but Gertie suspected she would prove no different from her older sisters. Oddly enough, the Baron Barclay remained a decent man, honest and faithful to his wife. Though Alexander had no attachment to any of the Barclays, Gertie had found the younger Barclay to be modest and agreeable.

Not at all like his brother.

Squaring her shoulders, she made her way down the stairs and into her alcove. As Penelope had said, Hephaestus waited for her. He wore only his breeches and his mask. The candlelight flickered across the planes of his pectorals, and Gertie could not help but admire the ridges of his muscled chest. He stood in attentive silence. She circled her prey. An exciting eagerness budded within her, but the Lady Athena must always be calm and contained.

"You have returned," she remarked with nonchalance.

"But of course," he replied. "Lady Athena."

"You may come to regret your decision."

"Is it your intent to make me regret, Lady Athena?"

She narrowed her eyes at him. "A good servant would not ask such an improper question. In forewarning you, I am exhibiting a measure of benevolence. Do not tax my generosity."

"Your charity is unnecessary, Lady Athena."

She inhaled sharply. They had been together all of five minutes and already he was beginning to ruffle her. "I speak because you do not appear to have benefitted from your punishment."

"Then punish me again if you wish. My body is yours."

His words made her shiver.

"Very well. Let us see how well you follow orders."

She went to her writing table and opened the drawer to remove a wooden paddle. Lance, having seen her punishment of Hephaestus the other night, had offered it to her.

Hephaestus took in the paddle but showed no emotion.

"Brace yourself against the table," she told him. She thought of having him shed his breeches once more, but the sight of him half-naked was sufficient to stir a warm agitation within her.

He did as told. Grasping the handle of the paddle with both hands, she swung it against his buttocks.

"Well done," he praised, "but I know you capable of more, Lady Athena."

Warmth surged inside her. He made a mockery of her. She failed to understand him, his purpose in seeking her out and provoking her into punishing him. Well, Lady Athena would not be underestimated,

The image of Phineas Barclay flashed in her mind. If only Lady Lowry could be Lady Athena always. Barclay would not have dared to speak with such audacity to Lady Athena. Or if he were to be such a fool, instead of scurrying away in defeat, she would have made him cower, made him repent his impertinence. Strange, but Lord Barclay seemed to inspire more anger in her than did the intelligence of her husband's mistress. Perhaps it was easier to direct her fury towards him than at her husband. Her private conversation with Lord Barclay had been more embarrassing to her than any public disdain she had received from Alexander.

Barclay's eyes, twinkling with merriment, haunted her even now. They pulled at her with an inexplicable gravity, and she found herself falling into their sapphire depths. They were beautiful eyes, fringed with dark golden lashes. The gods had been too kind to him. Lady Athena would not have stood for such injustice. Lady Athena would have...

Gertie stopped, suddenly aware that she had been walloping his backside quite hard. He should have made a sound or some movement to snap her from her trance. Stilling the shaking of her hand, she went to stand in front of him.

He looked up at her. "Thank you, Lady Athena."

She breathed a sigh of relief. Their gazes met through their masks, and it seemed his eyes invited her. She felt an uncomfortable throb in her nether region. This would not be the first man to arouse the carnal urges within her, but his was a body that could have been sculpted by Michelangelo. She was tempted to slide her hands up over his shoulders and down the bulge of his upper arms. He had such shapely arms. She would have liked nothing more than to glide her hands along each and every muscle.

"You have a strange predilection for punishment," she said to distract herself from her feelings. "It is not the usual expectation here at the *Ballroom of Pleasures.*"

"I did not come to Madame Botreaux's seeking punishment," he replied. "I favor the cries of ecstasy I am able to wring from the women I *pleasure* and would be pleased to demonstrate upon your ladyship."

Her breath caught in her throat. Ignoring the effect, she went to return the paddle. "That is a privilege that must be earned."

"Has no one earned such a privilege with you, Lady Athena?"

"No."

"And why do you make yourself suffer such failures, Lady Athena?"

She pressed her lips into a line. "I suffer nothing."

"Are you unfamiliar with the sublime elation of *orgasmos*, of your body wracked with uncontrollable delight?"

"Do you mean to imply that I have never spent?" she evaded.

"Many women have not," he stated plainly. "Or they may know some lesser form but have not had pleasure wrung from their bodies until they can bear no more."

Her cunnie pulsed at his words. She knew the lesser form, and only from pleasuring herself. But she had heard the ecstatic cries of other women in the *Ballroom* with undeniable envy. She had often wondered what it would be like to experience their bliss.

"Why deny yourself, Lady Athena?" he asked. "Should you not expect—nay, demand—that your lovers service you and bring you the pleasure you deserve?"

Her lower lip trembled. She could feel her body yearning towards him. Would it be so terrible if she had him…

No! She could feel the power of Lady Athena slipping.

"Be it cries of delight that you seek?" she asked him. She strode from her alcove and motioned for one of the maidservants. She directed the young woman to lie upon the chaise and lift her skirts.

"You will service her—with your hands behind you," Gertie informed Hephaestus.

He smiled. "Hardly a challenge, Lady Athena."

Gertie shook her head as he shuffled on his knees to the other woman, whom he instructed, "Come closer towards me, m'dear."

The blushing maid slouched down, pulled up her skirts and spread her legs. Positioning himself between her thighs, he leaned in towards her mons. Taking a seat in the chair nearby, Gertie folded her arms across her chest and watched as he lightly tongued the pink flesh before him. His tongue circled the folds, gently urging the nub of flesh between them to protrude. The woman closed her eyes, a peaceful murmur escaping her lips. Her body relaxed against the chaise. He took his time with slow thorough licks, his tongue a brush against her canvas. His languid strokes against her clitoris drew long low moans from the woman. Gertie had never seen such a look of contentment—the kind worn after an itch had been scratched or after tasting the sweetness of a ripe summer berry.

The warmth in Gertie's loins had spread to every limb, but she remained motionless as she watched. He was staring at her over the body of the woman. His eyes seemed to say, "I could be doing this to you." A shiver went up her spine.

Gradually he quickened the pace of his fondling. At times his tongue would slip below and dart into her cunnie, eliciting a delighted gasp. Gertie marveled at the stamina of his tongue. He wielded it as if it were his erection. He plunged his tongue further into the woman, and from the hysterical sounds coming from the woman, Gertie imagined his tongue to be doing all manner of feats within her. Gertie felt her own body straining in unison with the woman on the chaise. Her own clitoris throbbed for attention. The woman began to spasm on the chaise, but he did not stop his tongue until the majority of the woman's wailing had waned. With tender caresses, he eased her down from her orgasm.

Gertie closed her eyes and cursed the other woman, then herself. Her hand had itched to fondle her own clitoris, to seek relief and some semblance of the pleasure experienced by the redhead.

Instead, her body remained as tense as a violin chord over-strung. And though it had been her idea to bring in the other woman, she could not help but feel that she had played into his hands. She glanced at him, but his expression was not one of triumphant smugness. He gazed at her without emotion, waiting for her next command.

"You may leave us," Gertie told the maid.

"Thank you, Lady Athena, thank you," the maid said with a grateful bow. "If you require my presence again…"

I will not, Gertie thought silently.

When the woman had left, she turned back to Hephaestus. The lower half of his face glistened with the other woman's cunt juices. Gertie felt a flare of jealousy. Her desire to test him had faded, and she now found herself wondering what to do with him next.

* * * * *

Phineas set down his morning coffee and attempted to read the *Times* his butler had handed him, but his mind kept drifting back to last night. Back to the *Ballroom of Pleasures*. Back to Lady Athena. She had looked quite magnificent in her flaming red corset. Penelope had told him that much of Lady Athena's attire were of her own designs. He liked her creativity and her boldness. He even liked the fire that she cast at him through her glares. However, he was beginning to suspect that, despite all appearances, she was not as imposing as she pretended to be, even if she had given his arse a proper paddling. He shifted in his chair.

It made little sense why Lady Athena would punish herself by denying her body pleasure. She was not immune to arousal. He had seen that as he serviced the maid. Lady Athena had made no gesture, nor spoken a word, but he had detected the flush in her cheeks. And though his nose had been buried in the other woman, he could sense Lady Athena's arousal. He wondered if she had gone to seek relief in some other form, by herself or perhaps with another subject, someone she trusted. She certainly had left him abruptly last night, leaving him to wonder if their time together had come to an end.

"Master Robert is here," his butler announced.

"His Lordship, the Baron Barclay," Phineas corrected. "You are not so addlepated that you would forget his title, eh, Gibbons?"

"But you are—"

"I am not yet, and if I had it my way, my brother would remain Baron."

Gibbons inclined his head. "I have been some five and twenty years with the family. Old habits die hard, my lord."

"Especially when grounded in purposeful stubbornness. You may show my brother in."

The young man who entered the dining room resembled Phineas in eyes only. Robert Barclay had inherited the petite slender frame of their mother as well as her chestnut hair. Though he was still handsome as all the Barclay siblings were, he had developed more hollowness beneath the eyes in the five years that Phineas had been absent.

"I agree with Gibbons," Robert declared.

"You agree that he spent some five and twenty years in the service of our family or that old habits die hard?" Phineas returned.

His brother pressed his lips together before answering, "I agree that I am Master Robert. *You* are the Baron Barclay."

"Not yet, thank God. Coffee?"

Robert eyed the eggs and ham upon the dining table. "I had quite a large breakfast this morning. I think I shall not eat till supper."

"I do miss the hearty English breakfast," Phineas said as he cut into his ham. "How is a man to start the day properly on coffee and pastries alone?"

With a sigh, Robert sank into a chair at the table. "You need not wait to reclaim the barony. The paperwork is merely a formality."

"I did not return to England to reclaim the barony. My 'death' has worked out quite well in that regard."

"But you are the rightful baron and much better suited to the position than I!"

Phineas shook his head. "You have always been the upstanding Barclay, though our aptly named sister Prudence may best you yet. I am an irascible rake recovering from a scandalous duel, and as you and our dear friend Lord Bertram have reminded me: a second scandal would spell my doom. How am I better suited to the barony than you?"

Robert let out an exaggerated sigh. "Phineas, I have not the disposition for a Baron."

"That matters not. You have the capable Mr. Hancock to manage all affairs concerning the estate and its businesses—"

"Yes! And he will not stop speaking to me of the copper mine."

"How is Bettina? I have been in England over a fortnight and have yet to set eyes on my dear sister-in-law."

"She continues to caution me against my association with you."

"She is a sensible woman. You were quite right to marry her."

Robert watched in disbelief as Phineas buttered his bread nonchalantly. "Of course I told her that as you are *my brother*, I am bound to you."

"You did not have to procure this lovely apartment for me—or do you mean it as an inducement if I take back the barony?" Phineas asked with amusement before biting into his toast.

"I would do better to heed her advice and leave you to your own devices!" cried Robert.

"You would. May I recommend that you listen to your wife more often?"

"Phineas, I would that you would stop your jesting! Hancock is most insistent on this matter regarding the mine."

"What of our mine?"

"Apparently there is evidence of a significant copper load down one of the tunnels, but to access it, we must bore below Lowry land. The steward for Lowry likes us even less than the Earl himself. Hancock will have no success talking to him. I have attempted to bring up the matter with Alexander, but he refuses to engage."

"Not surprisingly. I doubt Alexander takes much of an interest in the business of his estate."

"Even if he did, I have not the skill in persuasion."

"I would be worse. I am convinced the man loathes me."

"Well, Hancock did relay a new bit of information. Apparently, the Lowry steward consults not with the Earl but with his wife."

Phineas looked up from his plate. "The Countess?"

"Yes, and I thought...well, since you have a way with the fair sex..."

"I would not raise my hopes. I think she may loathe me more

than her husband at present."

"How is that possible? She barely knows you."

"I made a rather impertinent remark to her at the Bennington ball."

His brother's face fell. "In God's name, what could you have possibly said?"

"You have no wish to know."

Robert's frown deepened. "And *what* compelled you to say what you did?"

Phineas contemplated. "I had no intention to vex her, though it was clear to me afterwards that she did not take to my suggestion warmly, but I confess a part of me wished to confront her after she had clearly demonstrated her disdain of me, and I had yet to make her acquaintance."

"She is a Farrington or had you forgotten in your absence how much they dislike us?"

"They are not all as scornful as you think," Phineas replied, recalling how easily Sarah Farrington had responded to him.

"And since when do you give a damn if someone should spurn you? You and Abigail have always done as you please without a care for what others have thought of you, and Georgina following in your footsteps. If I had the nonchalance the two of you possess, I should be quite the cheerful man, I assure you!"

"A dreadful prospect."

Robert threw up his hands. He reached for a slice of toast and began to butter it furiously. Phineas watched his brother with sympathy and a twinge of remorse. Robert had inherited the barony at four and twenty, a young age for a man of his tender disposition. Certainly the circumstances could not have been more distressing. Nonetheless, Phineas would not have allowed the barony to remain with Robert if he had not thought his brother capable.

"Tell me more about the Countess of Lowry."

"What of her?" Robert replied with a mouthful of bread.

"Have we met her before?"

"I think not. Her family is quite bourgeois."

"She is familiar to me somehow."

"You have lain with so many women, I wonder that the entire sex is not familiar to you?"

"You may be a cheerless man, but let it not be said that you have lost your humor."

"I have no opinion of the Countess of Lowry."

"Why not?"

"Should I?"

Phineas recalled what Mrs. Pemberly had offered in the way of opinion.

"Why an interest in the Lady Lowry?" Robert asked.

"If I am to broach the matter of the mine with her, I should like to better understand her temperament."

Robert perked up. "Well, our paths do not often cross, but she is mostly reserved the occasions I have seen her. She did not seem to be particularly disagreeable. I attended the wedding, and she was cordial enough. Do you truly intend to speak with her?"

"It is the least I can do to relieve some of the burden you have had to shoulder in my absence."

"Yes."

The little word was spoken with great relief. Phineas realized he would have to do more to assist his younger brother.

"But what if she will not see you?" Robert asked, his brow furrowed. "You said that you had vexed her."

"That will pose a challenge but not an insurmountable one."

Finishing his coffee, Phineas decided that he would send his card to Lowry House that day to request an audience with the Lady Lowry.

CHAPTER FOUR

"I HAVE NO DESIRE to grant him an audience today," Gertie informed the Lowry butler as she donned her bonnet. "Nor do I expect to have a change of heart the morrow."

"Lord Barclay will ask, as he has done the past dozen times, if you would—" the man began.

"He may ask a hundred times, the answer shall be the same," Gertie declared as she buttoned her riding jacket over her olive green gown.

The butler hung his head. "Very well, your ladyship."

Gertie regretted her curtness with the butler, but she could not help but be cross whenever she had to think of that Phineas Barclay. Perhaps she needed to pay a visit to the *Ballroom* to relieve her nerves. It had been a sennight since last she went, attempting to dispel the anguish over Alexander and his mistress. Although the anguish remained, Hephaestus did provide some relief in the form of a distraction. She had been tempted to return earlier, curious to learn whether he had given up on Lady Athena, but she wanted some distance between them, some time to recapture her old form. Perhaps he would have moved on in her absence, and she would be relieved by it—and a little sorrowful. But it would prove much safer if they parted ways. She could not shake the suspicion that he was up to something.

"Perhaps my lady would like one of her maids to ride along?" the footman inquired when her horse had been brought around to the front of the house.

"I would keep them unnecessarily from their tasks," Gertie answered as she stepped onto the footstool and mounted the steed. "I can manage quite well on my own."

Taking the reins, she barely managed to guide the horse beyond the square when a voice stopped her. At first she thought it was Hephaestus, and her heart nearly stopped. She had been discovered! But how?

She turned around slowly and saw instead Lord Barclay, mounted gloriously on a trotter. With his graceful posture and smart attire—a French striped coat with square tails and black bicorn—he cut a most gallant figure.

"Good day, Lady Lowry," he greeted.

The most simple words throbbed with sensuality when spoken by him. Gertie straightened her back and prepared her armor.

"I fear I am indisposed at the moment," she replied. "I have an engagement to keep."

He looked around her. "You are riding sans a chaperone?"

"I am no young maid but a married woman of many years."

"You have six and twenty years—hardly an old matron."

She ground her teeth. For some reason it irked her that he knew her age, but then there was little that did not irk her with Lord Barclay.

"I should be delighted to accompany you to your destination."

Her eyes widened before she could stop them. The last thing she desired was his company! Glancing towards the sun, she saw that the day was much later than she had hoped, and she did not wish to keep little Peggy waiting.

"That will not be necessary," she informed him. Of all people, Lord Barclay would be the least qualified to serve as a woman's chaperone!

As if reading her mind, he said, "Any indignity of our riding together would be mitigated as you are a married woman of many years."

"I am in some hurry."

"Where do you go, m' lady?"

Gertie shifted in her seat, causing her horse to scamper in its place. Wanting an end to their conversation, she replied truthfully, "St. Giles."

"The parish?"

"Yes, and if you would be a gentleman, I should like to delay no longer."

He frowned. "You cannot venture to St. Giles alone."

"I can manage quite well on my own," she snapped. "I have been there many times before *alone*."

"I would be a poor gentleman if I allowed you there."

"Thankfully I do not require your permission."

She urged her horse forward.

"Then you will have to suffer my company," he said, reigning his horse next to hers.

Gertie bristled, but there was little she could do if she intended to keep her engagement. They rode in silence for most of the way—which baffled her since he had sought her audience. Now that he had the opportunity to speak with her, he said nothing. How perturbing this man was!

She allowed herself one glance in his direction when she thought he wasn't looking. He seemed perfectly at ease, content to be accompanying her as if they were out for a spring ride in the woodlands instead of heading into one of London's poorest parishes. The only time he appeared bothered was when the stench of human waste and refuse that had been tossed out the windows proved too much. He had pulled out a scented handkerchief to cover his nose. Despite the hour, they passed a tavern where two men lay prone in the streets, sleeping off the effects of rot-gut gin.

They stopped before a two-storied building in need of a new roof. Most of its windows had lost at least one if not both shutters. A faded wooden sign above the door read *Orphan Asylum for Girls*. Gertie dismounted before Barclay could offer to assist her and rang the bell. She turned to inform Lord Barclay that she would be a while, but he, too, had dismounted.

An older woman opened the door and showed them into a small parlor. Gertie sat upon the settee. Barclay, after a skeptical review of the furniture, opted to remain standing. A short, stout gentleman whose grey hairline cut a crescent at the top of his head entered the room, followed by a gaggle of little girls. Gertie smiled upon seeing their delighted faces. Her friend Harrietta, the Marchioness of Dunnesford, had introduced her to the orphanage. They would often come together, but now that the Marchioness had a child of her own and spent more of her time at Dunnesford, Gertie had taken to visiting the orphanage by herself.

"Lady Lowry," greeted Mr. Winters, the founder of the orphan asylum. He noticed Barclay. "Ah, this must be your husband, the Earl?"

Gertie flushed as she watched the man bow obsequiously before Barclay.

"This is the Baron Barclay," she supplied. "A close relation."

Without looking, she could feel Barclay's brows rise in amusement for he no doubt remembered that she had described him as a *distant* cousin at the Bennington ball.

"Welcome, sir," Mr. Winters said. "I am Mr. Winters. May I offer you some tea?"

"Thank you, no," Gertie answered for the both of them. This would have to be one of her shorter visits.

"Lady Lowry, Lady Lowry!" a couple of girls chanted. "I have sewn the lace you gave us to my cap!"

"'ave you brought us a treat?" asked a girl with freckles splashed across her nose.

"Catherine!" Mr. Winters chided.

"Of course!" Gertie replied as she pulled a small satchel of confections from her reticule.

The girls squealed and thrust their eager hands before her. The room fell silent save for the sounds of chomping.

"Aw come we ain't seen you afore?" one of the girls asked Barclay.

"Maggie, that is no way to address a gentleman," Mr. Winters admonished.

"I confess I knew not the existence of this place before today," Barclay replied with ease.

"What sort of relation are you to Lady Lowry?" Catherine inquired.

Gertie interjected, "Tell me, girls, what activities you have engaged in this week? Did you like the books Lady Aubrey sent you?"

"Aw like your garments," Maggie said to Barclay. "Aw 'ave a drawing of a prince in one of me books. You look as if you could be a prince."

Barclay gave her a warm smile.

"A prince who dances with the princess," supplied another girl.

"Do you dance, sir?"

"When the occasion arises," he answered.

"It is not often that these girls meet a gentleman," Mr. Winters apologized. "If you should find them taxing."

"You are to be applauded for fostering such inquisitive minds."

Gertie stared at Barclay, surprised and reluctantly impressed by his patience.

"I should dearly like to learn to dance," sighed Catherine, "and to attend a ball! Like Cendrillon!"

"A minuet!" added another girl.

"Is it very hard to dance the minuet, Lady Lowry?"

"Not particularly difficult," Gertie said.

"Can you show us?"

Gertie hesitated.

The girls jumped up and down. "Show us! Show us!"

"Very well," said Gertie, rising to her feet. She turned to Mr. Winters, who shook his head.

"I have not danced in too many years," he explained.

"With the prince!" Maggie cried.

"Yes! Yes! With Lord Barclay!" the girls shouted as they clapped.

Gertie stole a glance at Barclay, who did not appear averse to the idea. He stepped towards her and bowed. She looked at the hand he presented to her. Not wanting to disappoint the girls, she placed her own hand in his. He grasped her hand firmly and gently led her to the center of the room.

"It is rather difficult without the music," she began.

"First you perform the honors," Barclay told them. He bowed to the girls, then to her. "A basic step consists of four steps in six beats of music."

They demonstrated starting with a plié on the left foot, rising to the ball of the right foot before straightening the legs and bringing their heels together. The motion was repeated starting with the opposite foot. They stepped forward, then sank into a plié.

The girls applauded. "Once more! Once more!"

Gertie felt the pronounced thudding of her heart against her chest. Barclay sought her gaze for permission. She nodded. He turned her around and they repeated the steps in the opposite direction. His hand felt warm and comforting about hers. He would not lead her astray and seemed to imbue her with his own grace and elegance, the hallmark of the minuet. When they finished and performed the honors, her head felt light, giddy with accomplishment.

"How marvelously lovely!" Catherine exclaimed. "How I wish I could dance the minuet!"

"Would you do me the honor then, my lady?" Barclay asked with a sweeping bow.

This threw the girls into another frenzy. The flush upon Catherine's face was so deep, her freckles disappeared, but she executed a curtsy and eagerly put her little hand in his. Glad for the respite, Gertie sat back to watch Barclay as he instructed Catherine on the steps. After Catherine, many of the others wanted a turn. He humored each and every one of them and proved a skilled dance master. Soon the room was filled with girls dancing the minuet.

The smiles and giggles made Gertie glow. A part of her frost towards Barclay thawed, though in truth, it had begun to the instant he took her hand for the minuet and stared into her eyes as if he had wanted to dance with her. How that could be when she as good as loathed the man stunned her. That same hand had fondled Sarah Farrington, had drawn cries of ecstasy, and the memory both disconcerted and excited Gertie. She could not keep her mind from wondering how his hand would feel upon her own body.

It was deucedly unfair that a man of his sort should have such powers to charm. Even the little ones fell victim to his spell, Gertie noticed wryly as the girls argued over who would have a second dance with Barclay.

"That is quite enough," Mr. Winters pronounced, eliciting a chorus of moans. "If Lord Barclay is amenable, I should like to show him the grounds."

Barclay surprised her by accepting the invitation. The girls followed. Gertie shook her head at how quickly they had forgotten her in favor of their 'prince,' but smiled at how much they had enjoyed their dancing. Foregoing the tour, she made her way upstairs to the nursery, where she found Mrs. Devon, a wet nurse who had worked in the orphan asylum for over twenty years, in the midst of swaddling a thrashing babe.

"I was about to bathe the wee one when Peggy awoke from her slumber cross as can be," Mrs. Devon explained. "I fed her but still she hollers."

Gertie took the howling babe from Mrs. Devon and paced about the room as she bounced the child in her arms. Peggy had been in the asylum three months. A man had delivered her here after finding her in a dwelling that had caught fire from an unattended hearth. Peggy had been badly burned, and Gertie's heart broke upon seeing the charred skin. They had bathed her in ointments and salves to ease the blisters. Her skin was finally beginning to heal, but she still had patches of red and white. Nonetheless, Gertie thought her beautiful.

With Peggy occupied, Mrs. Devon was able to tend to the other infants. Gertie sang to little Peggy, eventually seating herself in a rocking chair. After sucking on Gertie's finger, Peggy drifted into sleep. How calming the warm little bundle felt in her arms, Gertie reveled as she stared down at the small splotchy face. She imagined that she would never tire of holding Peggy. She would be content and want for nothing more if only she could have a Peggy for her own. Even the mighty Lady Athena would bow to such a sweet creature.

Feeling eyes upon her, Gertie looked up. Lord Barclay stood upon the threshold. How long had he been there? she wondered.

"It grows dark soon, my lady," he informed her, his voice low as not to wake the sleeping babes.

Gertie nodded. Rising, she reluctantly returned Peggy to Mrs. Devon. Downstairs in the parlor, the girls clamored for Lord Barclay to return.

"You will bring him again, will you not?" Catherine begged Gertie.

"Will you show us another dance next time?" another asked.

"Well, I—I suspect Lord Barclay is a busy man," Gertie stuttered.

"On the contrary, my schedule is quite open," Barclay supplied.

Gertie bristled for he seemed amused to gainsay her. "Let us—we shall see then, my darlings."

Barclay bid adieu with a gallant leg to the little girls, who gathered at the door to wave to them and see them off until their horses rounded the block and went out of view. Silence descended once again between them. Gertie decided to fill the void.

"It was…kind of you to learn the girls how to dance."

"It would have been unseemly to deny such eager students."

"You have a—you have endeared them to you. I confess I thought your charms reserved for…" She could not finish the thought as the memory of him and Sarah came to mind.

"I have two younger sisters," he explained. "Prudence, the youngest, is nearly twenty years my junior."

"Ah. I have not met her. She has not had her come-out, I take it?"

"Another year. She is in no hurry, though I would merit her with having the greatest maturity amongst us Barclays despite her years."

"I should have liked to have had a sister," Gertie thought aloud. "A younger one."

"You have many at the asylum."

"Yes, though I feel more like a doddering aunt to them at times. They are quite *lively*."

"I have no doubt they could eat a man alive with the voracity of a pack of wolves," he reflected.

Gertie chuckled. "They would not eat you alive. You have entranced them—like a snake charmer."

He studied her. "Somehow I think I am at once the charmer and the snake?"

"Yes, well…there is the matter of your repute, sir. Alas, you have a way with the fair sex, young and old—or so I am told."

And witnessed. Gertie scolded herself for surely she had given him an opening to make a spiteful remark as he had that night at the ball.

"And you have a way with the littlest ones," he said. "The one named Peggy—she suits you."

Perhaps she was nearing her menses, when maudlin sentiments could overcome her, for she nearly choked at hearing his words. She had never told anyone how much she longed for a child of her own. For a man she barely knew to have come close to touching that chord was too much.

"She survived a horrific fire," she explained, feeling safer discussing the babe. "She was apparently alone, and whoever cared for her did not return to claim her."

"Hers is a cruel world."

"Yes, but what I have learned from the girls at the asylum is that children are remarkable creatures. They are driven to be happy, their resiliency unmatched. Their presence invigorates me."

"Indeed? I think they have drained me completely of my vigor."

An inadvertent laugh escaped her lips. "All the better, that you may wreak less of your mischief."

She caught herself voicing her thoughts aloud and quickly added, "In truth, I find the girls tiring at times as well."

But he would not be diverted so easily. "And you disapprove of my 'mischief.'"

She caught her lower lip beneath her teeth. To her surprise, she was enjoying her tête-à-tête with him and had no wish to be reminded of their night at the Bennington ball.

"Of course," she replied.

"Why?"

"Who does not?"

"Is it so hard a question for you to answer?"

She narrowed her eyes at him. "The mark of a self-absorbed man is one who insists the conversation revolve around him."

Turning up her nose, she quickened the pace of her horse. But he matched her and grabbed her reins, forcing her to turn and face him.

"If you disapprove, why did you watch us?"

Her heart began to beat rapidly, and she had to force herself not to look away from his intense stare.

"You came into the room of a sudden," she threw at him.

"You did not have to hide and…observe."

"I did not…" She felt herself turn red. "I hid only because…oh, you are an insufferable man!"

To add insult to injury, he threw his head back and laughed. "I have had much worse said of me, madam."

"I am sure you have!" she snapped with a tug of the reins.

"Do not mistake that I disapprove of your Peeping Tom. I understand its titillation."

She sucked in an incredulous breath. "You overstep your

bounds, my lord, if you think I am a woman who would discuss such matters with you!"

She jerked her reins free from her hand. Fortunately, Lowry House was just around the corner.

"You prefer dialogue with Alexander."

"Decent folk would not—"

The specter of Lady Athena would not allow her to finish her sentence.

"Forgive me, but many a decent folk are dreadfully tedious."

"Yes, well—I mean—no. Of course a cad like you would find decency dull."

"And certain 'decent' persons are not what they seem."

"And you would know?" she asked archly as she pulled up before the house and slid off the horse before he could offer her assistance.

"The benefit of what you term my 'mischief' is that I have come to know a great many people, most of whom are not what they seem."

She was not looking at him, but she felt his gaze boring into her as he meant to unearth her secrets.

"How ironic," she declared, "for you are exactly what you seem. Good evening, sir!"

To her relief, the butler had seen her approach and opened the door. She did not have to hear Barclay's rebuttal before entering the sanctuary of her own home.

"Are you well, my lady?" the butler inquired as she untied the ribbon of her bonnet with trembling hands.

"Yes, yes," she lied.

Upstairs in her boudoir, she took several deep breaths. She ought not to let that Lord Barclay disconcert her so. He was not worth the agitation, even if the girls at the asylum did enjoy his company. She had spoken true when she said that he was what he seemed, but he also seemed *more* than her initial judgment of him. She tried to envision Alexander at the asylum, and concluded that her husband would never have had the patience to deal with the girls. He would not have accompanied her to the asylum in the first place. Alexander did not even venture to ask where she went on her Wednesdays.

As she removed her riding jacket, Gertie realized that Barclay had not broached his topic with her. Surely all his requests for her audience was not about the *Orphan Asylum*? Having stayed at the asylum longer than she had intended, Gertie quickly changed into her evening attire and went downstairs to dinner. She hoped Alexander would not be put out by her tardiness.

"I will be dining at White's with Millington," he informed her when she came across him in the hallway.

Millington was a classmate of his from Eton, but she happened to know that Millington had left for Bath yesterday for she had overheard Millington's mother discussing the trip with the Dowager. Alexander, however, did not know that Gertie knew.

He was off to see his mistress, she realized. She wondered who it was. Was the woman pretty? Of course she was. How long had Alexander had this mistress?

But the answers would serve her no purpose, so she let Alexander by without a word. She decided that night she would return to *Madame Botreaux's*.

CHAPTER FIVE

The pounding in his ears intensified as Phinease held back his arousal. Standing before him in her scarlet corset, Lady Athena nudged him with her boot. She had him on his knees again, this time using his hands. But for nothing so enticing as licking cunnie. Rather, he shone her black boots with a rag.

He had returned every night to the *Ballroom* to await her. For a sennight, she did not show.

"Do not flatter yourself," Penelope had told him when he voiced his concern that perhaps he had caused her disappearance. "I doubt that the world of Lady Athena centers around the *Ballroom*—or you."

He had often speculated who Lady Athena personified in the world above the *Ballroom*. He had studied the women of London, wondering with each one if she might be the glorious Lady Athena, but none were obvious suspects. Lady Athena was bold, strong, confident, and *electrifying*. He felt his senses come alive in her presence. No woman in the world outside the *Ballroom* produced such a surge in his body. He could attribute the thrill to the hunt, his desire to conquer the warrior-goddess, but his days at the *Ballroom* without her had proved how keenly he awaited her. When he was not thinking of Lady Athena, his thoughts turned oddly to the Countess of Lowry.

"You may rise," she commanded when her boots gleamed even in the dim lighting.

When he was upright, she did nothing but stare at him, as if she knew not what to do with him next.

"Have I earned the privilege of pleasuring Lady Athena?" he prompted.

She hesitated as she considered his proposition. He could hardly contain his triumph when she replied, "Perhaps a little."

She pushed her breasts up with her hands. The voluptuous orbs filled his vision.

"Fondle them, Hephaestus.."

At last she would allow him to touch her! Slowly, he reached to cup a breast with reverence. Her breath caught when he passed his thumb over the nipple. He sank his digits gently into her rounded flesh. She felt glorious.

He leaned into her bosom and flicked his tongue at a nipple, making her gasp. When he had teased both nipples to pointed hardness, he encased one in his mouth and sucked. She moaned her approval. He sucked harder. She thrust the breast further into his face. He pulled as much of the flesh into his mouth as he could, suckling her tit with increasing vigor. The length of his desire pulsed.

"Enough," she ordered before he could lavish the same attention upon her other breast, which bore a small birthmark left of the nipple.

She lowered her gaze to his crotch, where his desire tented the fall. With some hesitation, she put her hand to his hardness, her breath uneven. His ardor stretched at her touch.

"Shall I allow you to pleasure yourself, I wonder?"

"No," he replied resolutely. "Until my lady has found pleasure, I would not be worthy."

She released him. "Suit yourself."

His gaze caressed the contours of her body—the flare of her hips, the swell of her thighs. If she would but let him, he could worship her body.

As if sensing his thoughts, she asked, "Do you enjoy pleasuring women?"

"Without question. How do you prefer to take pleasure, Lady Athena?"

"I ask the questions," she told him. "In my observation, many men seek only their own satisfaction."

"They forego a great deal of pleasure then."

"Do you suggest that you are different?"

"Perhaps my lady would like to ascertain the truth for herself?"

She colored. "How might you pleasure a woman?"

"The young maid you had me pleasure with my tongue," he

answered as he held her gaze, "I would have gladly done to…"

You.

"My lady," he finished.

Her chest rose with inflated breath as she perhaps remembered his performance. She began to pace in front of him. "Tell me of your last lover."

Phineas recalled the Marquise de Dupray, a lovely woman with dark black hair, who had an affinity for being the voyeur, not unlike the Lady Athena. "A French Marquise. She liked to watch me as I instructed her damsels on the finer points of pleasure."

"Damsels?"

"The young maids in her employ. She preferred them virginal."

He could not tell if his answer displeased her, but she nodded for him to continue.

"Her chamber had a large bergere armchair. She would sit in that chair and fondle herself as she watched us."

"What did she have you do?"

"Fuck."

He had spoken the word clearly, but she started as if she had not quite discerned his answer.

"I would ravish the maid," he elaborated, speaking at a slower tempo so that she would miss not a word. His arousal reared its head with the memory. "The Marquise would have me take her maids in all manner of positions: standing, sitting, kneeling."

"Describe one such instance."

He thought he detected a slight hitch in her voice, but her face evinced no emotion.

"Madame had a Dutch scullery maid, Katrien, whom she favored. One night Madame called Katrien to her chambers. I undressed Katrien, removing every last article including her garters and stockings. Madame then told her to kneel and take my shaft into mouth. Katrien had a remarkably pliant mouth, though when she first came to work for Madame, she often gagged while taking a man's member. She took almost the entire length of me down her throat this time."

Lady Athena had stopped pacing, her gaze upon his crotch.

"Madame would sit in that chair of hers and urge me to thrust into Katrien harder, to grab Katrien by the hair and speed her motion on my shaft. When I spent, Madame wanted Katrien to swallow every last drop of seed. Once, Katrien coughed, and my seed spilled from her lips onto the ground. Madame was furious and made Katrien sleep on a pallet she kept next to her bed."

He watched as Lady Athena reached for his fall. "Have you ever been treated such, my Hephaestus? Like a pup to be taught a lesson?"

'*My* Hephaestus' she had said. Encouraged, he answered with a "no" but gave her such a look as to suggest that he would welcome such a prospect from her.

She smiled appreciatively and brushed her fingers over the tented area of his breeches. "Continue."

"Madame and I had trained Katrien well. She licked the last droplet and begged for more. That pleased Madame."

He paused to relish the feel of Lady Athena's fingers. The pleasure was almost unbearable. She undid his buttons, releasing the hardened member. She stared at his shaft for several beats before grasping it. Suppressing a satisfied moan, he returned to his story.

"I knelt behind Kat and entered her. My shaft hardened further inside her. Madame, aroused by the sight of us, spent first. Then Katrien spent."

"Then what?" Lady Athena blew into his ear. She had drawn her body close enough for him to feel her heat. His hands itched to caress her—her arms, her hips, her thighs. Her hand had wrapped itself entirely about his erection, briskly pumping him.

"Then I fucked Madame."

Her hand stopped. Her face was close enough to his that if he turned, his mouth could have brushed her cheek. He inhaled her scent, a fresh and subtle essence mixed with the musk of arousal that clung in the air of the *Ballroom*.

"How?"

"Against the wall, her legs wrapped about my hips as I held her aloft and pressed my member deep into."

She resumed her stroking of his member. She had a gentle but firm touch, enticing his arousal higher and higher until the tip tingled.

"Did she spend?"

"Yes."

The Marquise had been insatiable. They would often spend half the night making love. He added, "With such force that she bit into me. I bore the marks of her teeth upon my shoulder for many days."

When she stepped away from him, he could see she was in thought. She absently stroked his chest. Her tongue darted from her lips and grazed his nipples. He wished he could see her mouth and discern the shape of her lips, but she always stood with the lone candelabra to her back, leaving her face in constant shadow.

Then to his surprise, she sank to her knees. Grasping him, she guided the hard pole into her mouth. Phineas groaned at the exquisiteness of her wet, velvet mouth wrapped about him. Cradling his shaft on her tongue, she waited a moment before curling her tongue and giving it a long suck. Her tongue lapped at the underside of his shaft, finding that deliciously sensitive area right beneath the flare of the head. The pleasure shot down his thighs and swirled in his groin. Was the Lady Athena truly practiced in the art of taking a man into her mouth or did she have a natural flair for it? The warmth of her mouth fueled a heat that had already been stoked by her earlier stroking. Did she mean to reward him for his story? As she took his length deeper into her mouth, her hand cupped his sack and tugged his balls. He could feel his arousal boiling there. Her mouth moved relentlessly up and down his shaft.

"Lady Athena," he said. "I will not spend lest my lady has first been fulfilled."

She pulled her mouth off and looked up at him.

"You flatter yourself. Did you think I would have allowed you to spend?"

Rising to her feet with a smile, she grasped him in her hand. When her fingers slid over the head, a tremor went down his legs.

"Till next we meet," she said over her shoulder as she strode from the alcove.

He waited until she was gone before letting out a groan, feeling as if his body was a tautly stretched string in need of plucking. He wondered how Lady Athena would have reacted to the whole story of the Marquise, who, as much as she enjoyed commanding her maids, became a kitten who groveled at his feet and begged for him to ravish her. Shaking off his arousal, he, too, left the alcove. He would need to employ a more forceful approach for he suspected that time was not in his favor where Lady Athena was concerned.

CHAPTER SIX

H ER HORSE PAWED the ground, restless for his mistress to provide direction, but Gertie stalled as she contemplated the façade of the apartment of Phineas Barclay. She considered turning her horse back down the street, but she imagined the disappointment she would have to face if she arrived at the orphan asylum sans Lord Barclay—*again*, for she had paid a visit but yesterday on her own, only to be peppered by the girls with questions as to why Lord Barclay had not accompanied her. She remembered the jealousy brewing at each mention of his name. She loathed that such a repulsive feeling should nest itself in her bosom. Then she imagined the smiles that would blaze from their faces if he should come, and that made her mind.

There was the possibility Lord Barclay was not at home. She would still proceed to the asylum, but at least her conscience would be at ease in the knowledge that she had made a good attempt to seek him out. Of course, if she had been complete in her diligence, she could have sent him word in advance of her coming or written him a request for his company. But she was reminded of all the times he had requested her audience and been spurned. Now she wished she had been more gracious.

No matter. She was done with being disconcerted by this man. Recalling her most recent night at the *Ballroom*, she summoned the daring of Lady Athena. She could hardly believe that she had taken a man into her mouth. She had only done so once before, though she had witnessed the act many times within the walls of the *Ballroom*. She had always been intrigued by it, how wrong it seemed, how depraved, how provocative and titillating. But finally, Lady Athena had regained some of her old form over the impudent Hephaestus. Though she had been more aroused than she had ever been listening to him recount his story with the Marquise, such that she had rushed home afterwards so that she could dive her hand between her thighs and frig herself to completion, she had successfully maintained her composure with him.

Her horse neighed as if to prod her along. Accepting the encouragement from her grey, she dismounted and made her way to the black double doors.

"Is Lord Barclay home?" she asked of the butler who answered the door.

"Is he expecting you, my lady?"

"No, and I will not impose if he is occupied."

She began to turn on her heel.

"If you would but wait, my lady…" the butler urged, stepping aside to allow her passage. "Shall I see to your horse?"

"That won't be necessary. I will not be long."

"Would my lady care to wait in the drawing room?"

"I will not be long," she reiterated.

The butler began to take his leave but stopped to pick up a lace handkerchief.

"Yours, my lady?" he inquired.

She shook her head vigorously at the perfumed finery. As she waited for the butler to return, she tapped her riding crop into the palm of her other hand. The butler had not been astonished to find a woman calling upon his employer. No doubt he had seen many a woman crossing the threshold in his time.

She should not be surprised if Barclay declined to visit the orphan asylum. She knew of only one man besides Mr. Winters who had been there: the Marquess of Dunnesford. At first she had been rather intimidated by the man, but as she befriended the Marchioness, she came to know him as kindhearted and reasonable.

"You have a husband of perfection," she had once sighed to Harrietta, the Marchioness, upon learning that not only was Dunnesford a benefactor of the asylum but he and his wife had chosen to employ one of the girls.

"He is perfect for me," Harrietta had acknowledged.

"I am flattered," Vale had said, raising his wife's hand for a kiss, "but I am far from a perfect husband—if such a thing exists."

The man who descended the stairs would be the last candidate for a perfect husband. Despite that, she could not help a moment of awe as she observed Lord Barclay's dress. Attired in a marvelously embroidered waistcoat, breeches that molded his muscular legs, and the finest of linen, he presented a dashing vision. Gertie wondered how much time the man's toilette must absorb and did he go to bed in such a state of refinement?

"Lady Lowry," he greeted, "to what do I owe this pleasure?"

Strange but the man seemed genuine in his pleasure to see her.

"I will not occupy much of your time," Gertie said quickly. "I came only because the girls have such an interest in making your acquaintance again, but as I am sure you are engaged, I shall bid you good day."

He allowed her to make it all the way to the door before saying, "Stay."

She shivered at the command in his tone. Her heart betrayed her inner composure and quickened its beat. Turning, she saw him advancing towards her. His gaze pinned her to where she stood, and her better instincts failed her. A field mouse or any animal of *inferior* intelligence could have survived better than her at the moment.

Barclay drew up before her—much too close for comfort, and still she could not move. He looked down upon her, his voice low but free of smugness.

"You desire my company, Countess?"

"The girls," Gertie countered, fearing his body would take up all the air she needed to breath. "They wish to see you."

"Are you merely their messenger then?"

"Of course!" she snapped. The impudence of the man!

His lips curled in a half smile, and Gertie found herself fixated upon his mouth, recalling how those lips had planted themselves upon Sarah, wondering how they would feel upon her own body…

"You did not have to come," he pointed out.

"I was bound by my affection for…If you've no interest, sir— my lord, I will take my leave and trouble you no further."

"Did I say I had no interest?"

"I assumed…"

"Do you make a great many assumptions, Countess?"

"Are you always this impertinent?" she retorted, finding courage in her ire.

His smile broadened, the amusement twinkling into this eyes. To her relief, he stepped away from her. As he called for his butler, she inhaled a much needed breath.

"Gibbons, my hat and coat," Barclay instructed. He turned back to Gertie, this time speaking seriously. "I should be pleased to accompany you to the orphan asylum, Lady Lowry. I hope you will not hesitate to request my attendance anytime you venture into St. Giles."

"Are you offering yourself as a chaperone?" she asked, unable to fathom his chivalry to her.

"I doubt you have an interest in my fulfilling any other capacity," he stated as he donned his hat and gloves.

She flushed. "I would have no interest in you at all if not for the girls!"

"I rather doubt that."

He gestured for her to proceed before him. Grinding her teeth together, she gathered her skirts and swept past him. He was amusing himself at her expense, but she could not help her indignation and cursed herself for having sought him.

"Allow me," he said to his footman when Gertie prepared to mount her steed.

She bristled, envious of the independence men had when it came to mounting, but she stepped into his waiting hands. He lifted her into her saddle with ease.

Once more they began their ride in silence. She did not understand this man at all. One moment he was purposefully vexing her with language as his arsenal, the next he was dumb.

"You ought not feel obligated," she began.

He stared at her. "But of course I feel obligated, Countess. I could not disappoint the orphans."

Gertie knit her brows as she studied him. His words rang sincere. Could there possibly be a shred of kindness in him?

"I take it one of your assumptions of my character is that I am heartless?"

Damnation. How was he able to read her thoughts?

"Why should I think otherwise?" she returned.

"Because many men are not what they seem, even ones you would consider indecent."

"I merely thought that you would be busy—appointments with your tailor or bootmaker."

He smiled, amused once more. "Ah, you think me heartless *and* frivolous.''

"Are you not?" she challenged. "Have you a purpose, sir, beyond a well-turned cuff or the pursuit of a skirt?"

"No."

Expecting him to be a little sheepish, his brazen response surprised her. At the least, he was truthful, she granted him wryly.

"And you disapprove," he stated, providing her something more to respond to.

"Of course. Man was not gifted with intelligence and abilities that he may spend his time as a philanderer."

"You would rather I wile away my time at Brooks or White's with my own sex, indulging in smoke and drink, a good round of hazard, or a lively discussion of pugilism?"

"I do not disapprove of recreation but would rather men engage in useful pursuits. I wonder that we can allow such suffering as exists among our fellow man?"

"It would seem to me that when Man engages his intelligence and his abilities, he is wont to wreak destruction and suffering."

She shook her head. "That can be no excuse. You, sir, are clearly capable, intelligent, and possess certain skills that are perhaps best placed in a more deserving person. You could do much if you applied yourself."

For the first time, it seemed she had made him uncomfortable. He had no witty remark, no bold response.

"You overestimate my abilities," he said at last.

"I think not, but it would be a shame if your legacy was naught but that you excelled at debauchery."

"I have had no reason to care about my legacy. Why should I mind what is written upon my tombstone when I am dead?"

"And whilst you live?"

"Lady Lowry, you sound suspiciously of the Evangelical or Quaker faith."

"I am neither. My attendance to church has been wanting," she admitted.

"And mine horrific."

"How surprising," she said ironically.

He lifted an eyebrow. "Let he who is without sin cast the first stone."

She suppressed a smile. He had a disarming way about him. No wonder the women succumbed to him. She remembered how closely he had stood to her in the vestibule of his apartment. No man had desired to stand in such proximity to her. Did he possibly have an interest in seducing her or did he simply act in such a manner for effect?

As she expected, the girls at the asylum were thrilled to see their prince and dance master. He taught them steps from the cotillion and regaled them with stories of the French court and descriptions of Queen Marie Antoinette.

"Perhaps it is unwise for us to fill their minds with such glamour," Mr. Winters whispered to Gertie as the two observed how the girls hung upon Lord Barclay's every word. "But he brings them so much cheer, I've not the heart to stop it. You said he is a cousin of yours, my lady?"

"Of my husband."

"Pity he has spent such time traveling that he has not found a wife."

Gertie remained silent. There was no reason to divulge the reason for Lord Barclay's time on the Continent. As for a wife, she kept her thoughts to herself. She imagined Barclay had less a mind for a wife than his legacy.

After she had spent her time with little Peggy in the nursery, she and Barclay prepared to take their leave.

"When shall we see you again?" the girls clamored.

"I think they direct their question to you, sir," Gertie told Barclay with a grin. It was hard to stay jealous at him when he behaved so well with the girls.

Barclay looked at her, then turned to the girls. "If Lady Lowry will allow it, I should accompany her every Wednesday."

The girls flew to Gertie. "Oh, please! Lady Lowry, please! Do!"

She blinked several times as the situation sunk in. How could she possibly show without Lord Barclay now? She glanced towards Mr. Winters, but he proved of no help.

"Do, Lady Lowry, do say you will allow it!"

"I suppose..." she said.

The girls cheered and clapped their hands.

When she and Barclay were once again upon their horses headed home, she turned to him. "I hope you have not lifted their hopes only to disappoint them at a later time."

Surely he had no intention of visiting the asylum every week.

"And who else would escort you through St. Giles, m'lady?"

She stared at him, dumbfounded. Had he devised his response for the purpose of accompanying her? Why?

"As I have said, I need no escort," she said, refusing to accept his act of gallantry.

"Riding through St. Giles alone is most reckless, my dear Countess. I wonder that your husband allows it?"

She felt her bottom lip about to quiver. Alexander did not care enough to prohibit her from going.

"My husband is...*busy.*"

"At the races and card tables? At the very least, he should demand a groomsman—"

"It was my choice to discharge our groomsman."

"Ah, Alexander has been ineffectual at both horses and cards. Little has changed since last I saw him."

"He has been unlucky," she acknowledged, unsure why she should be defending her husband.

Barclay snorted. "He has forever been out of Fortune's graces then."

"Much to your satisfaction, I imagine!"

"Frankly, Countess, I worry more about my barber. The life of the Earl of Lowry concerns me not at all."

"It is common knowledge the disdain you bear the Farringtons."

"I haven't enough interest to disdain them, but I am sure their disposition is known to you."

She had to admit she would not be surprised at all if the disdain had first come from the Farrington side. And Sarah clearly did not disdain him. She suddenly remembered how in earnest he had sought her audience. What had it been in regards to? Did it no longer matter? If so, it was undoubtedly best that she not bring it up.

Curiosity, however, overcame her.

"Why did you wish to see me?" she blurted, then wondered in horror if he had perhaps wanted to talk to her about Sarah.

He eyed her through his quizzing glass. "I think that shall have to wait. You are far too vexed for critical dialogue."

"If I am vexed, it is because of you! If the Earl of Lowry affects you not, why did you want to speak with me? I demand to know! Lest it be in regards to my sister-in-law. I will not aid you in your efforts to seduce her."

"I think you have seen I require no aid in that realm."

Gertie felt her cheeks burn. "Then, pray tell, what concerned you enough to seek a meeting with me?"

"We can discuss the matter next Wednesday. May I suggest a riding habit of a different color? That shade of olive is less than complimentary upon you."

Her eyes widened. She had heard enough from others, but for him to remark upon her dress was too much. She pressed her lips together before saying through clenched teeth, "I can see why someone should wish to put a bullet through you."

"We dueled with swords," he corrected. "I should choose a more lively color for you."

"If you think I would take advice from a *murderer*, you are mistaken!"

The look of steel entering his eyes made her instantly regret her words, but she had felt trapped for she could not shake his presence on their journey home. It would be foolhardy to break into a gallop on the narrow cobbled streets, and she was not so skilled a rider that she could do so even on level ground.

His tone had lost its touch of amusement. He spoke slowly, "An' you think me such a monster, why do you allow me near the girls at the asylum?"

At first, she faltered in the face of his logic. As odious as she thought him to be, she could not bring herself to believe him evil.

"I would not," she finally decided, "had I a choice."

He shook his head. "It was in your power to decide otherwise. One always has a choice."

"I could not disappoint the girls."

"And if they wished to eat naught but cake and confections at every repast, you would not disappoint them?"

She sucked in her breath, bristling at his apt rejoinders, but then when she glanced at him, she chanced to imagine him a plumb cake and laughed. The humor returned to his face, brightening the sparkle of his eyes.

"You are a hundred times worse than the most deceitful of cakes," she said with a shake of her head, "and I am a fool to have allowed them to indulge such temptation."

"Thank you, I loathe to think I could not best a trifle or sugar plum."

A chuckle escaped her. This was madness. How could she engage in such banter with a man she had labeled a murderer but a moment ago? Granted, there were clearly circumstances surrounding his duel with Jonathan Weston that favored Lord Barclay somehow. Even the men serving as seconds for Weston had refused to implicate Barclay.

He was still a blatant debaucher. She should fear for her own repute if they were discovered to have spent such time together, but no one would seriously consider that Lord Barclay was attempting to seduce her. A wistful sigh rose within her. When they arrived at Lowry House, she almost wished the ride had not finished so quickly.

"Have you discharged your footman?" he commented when none of the servants arrived to greet them. He dismounted and came to her side before she could protest.

She had already begun to slide off her mount. He caught her at the waist and eased her to the ground. It was a natural action for him to take, and she did not think to accuse him of any impropriety, but the blood pounded madly between her ears. She found herself in such proximity to him that the brim of her hat could graze his face. Trapped between his body and that of the horse, she could manage no movement. She looked up at him and saw a quixotic intensity upon his features she had not seen before. Warmth flared through her body in response. She felt like she was about to be his prey, and it was the most intoxicating sensation. If he should lower his head to kiss her, she would not stop it.

Instead, he reached for the bridle behind her. "Allow me to see to your horse."

Dumbly, she nodded.

He bowed his head. "Until next Wednesday, Countess."

Tempering her disappointment, she nodded and walked up the steps. One of the maids answered the door, and Gertie swept inside without a backwards glance. Her heart continued to hammer at her chest. How she wished Harrietta were in town! She desperately needed a friend to help untangle the mess of thoughts swirling in her head. Alas, she had received a letter from the Marchioness this morning stating that she did not think her little one ready to make the journey to London and she could not bear to leave him.

"Was that Lord Barclay?" Sarah asked when Gertie had walked past the parlor that overlooked the entry to Lowry House.

"It was," Gertie answered curtly, not wishing to engage in dialogue.

"Does he mean to call upon us?" Sarah inquired eagerly.

"I think not."

She wanted solitude in her chambers, but Sarah continued to speak.

"Then...I don't understand. What is he doing here then?"

"He—he accompanied me on an errand."

"He accompanied *you*? Why?"

Gertie almost found herself replying *because he is a gentleman.* Which was an absurd consideration for a debaucher. But she had to admit that he did not have to escort her to St. Giles. *One always has a choice,* he had said.

To Sarah, she simply shrugged, saying, "I am not one to guess at his motives."

Sarah knit her brows, and Gertie could not help a small sense of triumph at Sarah's obvious jealousy.

"I heard he is wont to be capricious," Sarah said.

Gertie had not heard such a thing, but she merely nodded and took her leave. In the quiet of her own chambers, she replayed her last moment with Barclay. His nearness had been overpowering, yet exhilarating. It had been by chance, of course, that he stood so close to her. Yet the look in his eyes...Gertie shivered, recalling how a muscle along his jaw had twitched.

Agitated that she was proving to be no different than any other weak-willed quarry of his, she reached for her riding crop and called upon the powers of Lady Athena to shore her resolve. Then she remembered the handkerchief that she had seen at Lord Barclay's home.

It belonged to Sarah.

CHAPTER SEVEN

THE FARRINGTON WOMEN had taken leave of their senses, Phineas decided as he opened his door to admit Sarah. The Countess of Lowry suffered delusions that she could ride safely into St. Giles alone, and now Lady Sarah was risking her reputation calling upon him at his home during the day.

"Are you seeking to have me exiled, Lady Sarah?" he asked as he settled himself into a chair after seeing her seated on the settee of his drawing room.

"Nonsense. You and I both know Alexander has not the courage to demand satisfaction," she replied stiffly.

"There will come a time when he feels his hand has been forced."

"He cares not what I do. He only wishes to marry me off to some fat, old man that he can collect upon the dowry," Sarah said with biting bitterness.

"If he be a kind fat, old man, there are worse conditions."

"What a heartless man you are!"

He recalled the dialogue he had had earlier with Lady Lowry. The remonstrance from Sarah affected him not at all, but the accusations of the Countess had not fallen as lightly. Perhaps it was the emptiness of having spent five years on the Continent that had made him more susceptible to Lady Lowry's comments. He did not often associate himself with women of her character, though a woman like the Countess could easily be seduced into admitting her own hypocrisy.

Lacking in admirers, the Countess, despite her vociferousness, would ultimately be flattered by his attentions. He could see the sadness that she tried to hide from him, covering it with indignation over his audacity. He knew her marriage to Alexander to be unsatisfying but could not tell if she knew of his mistress. No doubt she did. But what could a woman do? Such was the tragedy of the fair sex when it came to matrimony. He would never place a woman in such a pitiless position.

He could have seduced her right there against her mount. She would not have offered much resistance. He could see it in her eyes, sense the tension in her body, smell her anticipation. Strangely, he had felt an urge to kiss her—and in full view of the Lowry House and its habitants. He remembered her full and supple lips, the rouge upon them wanting a little more application. With the proper aid, the Countess need not present herself quite so plain.

His body was tuned for sex, and it did not surprise him that he should respond to her arousal. Why he should care about how the Lady Lowry felt towards him was a more intriguing puzzle. The fact that he could seduce her into agreeing to the question of the mine did not escape him. Perhaps that was what Robert expected him to do. But he had no interest in pursuing that means to the end. The Countess warranted better than that.

"Have you lost your ability to speak?" Sarah's churlish voice intruded into his thoughts.

He eyed her with the notion to lay her across his lap and spank her. He had suspected she was a naughty girl in search of punishment. Last night, she had invited herself over. He trusted his servants to be discreet, but she had no such knowledge. Nonetheless, she had all but demanded he take her to bed. He had willingly done so, for his last session with the Lady Athena had left him aggravated.

Without bothering to release her from the confines of her gown, he had bent Sarah out his open window, threw up her skirts, and taken her from behind. The hour had been late, the candles in his room snuffed, but the moon had been out and an occasional patron of the alehouse around the corner stumbled by. He knew Sarah had enjoyed every minute of it.

He wondered if the Countess would have been similarly titillated. Would she be mortified or aroused that a passerby should look up and see her being fucked out the window? Both. Something about the Countess signaled to him that she was not as staid and boring as one might first believe. She was simply a field unplowed, a trail untraveled.

The image of the Countess being pummeled by his ardor as she hung halfway out his window made him shift uncomfortably in his seat.

"What business had you with my sister-in-law?" Sarah repeated.

"Business that does not concern you," he answered. "My dear, I think it unwise of you to come here."

She bristled.

"And safest if we conclude our *liaison*. I have no wish to tarnish your marital prospects."

He rose to his feet.

"But—"

As he pulled her to her feet, he kissed her hand. "May our families put aside their differences, as we two have."

"But—"

He led her to the door whilst she was still in shock.

"Until that day, Lady Sarah."

"But—"

In another moment he would have her out the door and he could return to this intriguing fantasy of the Countess, but just then his brother appeared.

"Lady Sarah!" Robert greeted in surprise.

Sarah flushed. Turning to Phineas, she attempted her most formal tone, "Good day to you, Lord Barclay."

"And to you," Phineas returned.

"It is the Lady Lowry that I asked you to speak with," Robert said when Sarah had left.

"I am aware," Phineas replied, heading to the sideboard in the drawing room. His thoughts of the Countess would have to wait.

"And? Have you spoken with her?"

"Have you five hundred pounds about you? Of course you have. You were always the miser of the family."

"What for? Is that what they propose to charge us for tunneling on their land?"

Phineas handed his brother a glass of sherry. "Take the five hundred pounds and issue it to the *Orphan Asylum for Girls* in St. Giles."

"Orphan asylum? Phineas, what are you about? Is that what the Countess demands from us?"

"No. It is your foray into philanthropy."

"My…? Phineas, explain yourself. Have you spoken with Lady Lowry?"

"Not of the mine."

"But you have spoken with her?"

Settling back into his chair with his own glass, Phineas recalled the rather enjoyable conversation with the Countess.

"Yes," Phineas relented. "You will be pleased to know that she now loathes me somewhat less."

"Jolly good. Then you will broach the subject of the mine when you next meet?"

"Perhaps. I have not yet won her over. My remark about her dismal selection in riding clothes put her off."

"Your…?"

Robert looked at his wine and downed it nearly one gulp. He shook his head. "I shall never understand you, Phineas."

"It would seem as if we were from different families instead of brothers," Phineas sympathized.

"I would I had never been 'adopted!'" Robert retorted. "There is no end to the farce in our family. First you–"

"Ah, dear Mama and Papa were first."

"And now Georgina and this wretched *crim con* of hers. Abigail wants me to escort Georgina to Vauxhall. Says it would do much to cheer her as they have a *menagerie*. But my wife will not be seen in her company. Perhaps you could…"

Phineas considered the challenge of going from Vauxhall to Madame Botreaux's. He had not yet missed a night at the *Ballroom* and had no intention of starting.

Seeing his brother's hesitation, Robert continued, "For bloody sake, Phineas, can you not put yourself to use?"

Phineas started, the words of the Countess ringing in his head. "Tell Georgina I cannot stay for long."

Robert nodded in gratitude. "Do you think the Countess will allow us access of the Lowry land?"

"I think so."

"I was right to have you talk with her then. Why was Lady

Sarah here?"

"You have no wish to know."

Robert sighed. Taking up his hat and gloves, he rose to his feet. "I hope you are not attempting to seduce the Countess of Lowry? I have no desire to incur the wrath of a Farrington if we are to tunnel beneath their land."

Phineas thought of the anger Sarah would no doubt experience when she emerged from her shock.

"I thought you intended I should use my arts of persuasion?" he replied.

Robert opened his mouth, but no words came to him. Phineas watched his brother depart, wondering when the poor chap would finally master the skill of ignoring his older brother. He finished off his wine, then proceeded upstairs to prepare for a night at the *Ballroom*.

* * * * *

Lady Athena found Hephaestus waiting for her in naked glory, per the instructions she had left for him. She had to pause to admire his sculpted body. He stood in full confidence of his nakedness, and she was reminded how unlike other men he was. But she refused to be taken by his attributes. She would not allow herself to tarry with him.

Tonight she wore her black ensemble with black fingerless gloves that went past her elbow. Tonight he would experience the strength of Lady Athena. Tonight he would not dare trifle with her.

"Pleasure yourself, Hephaestus," she told him.

Wordlessly, he gripped his shaft and coaxed it to hardness, all the while staring at her. She allowed him this impudence and even teased him by playing with one of her nipples, which protruded just above the top of her corset. She pinched her nipple, pulled it, twisted it. His member lengthened quickly in response. Striding over, she pressed a finger upon his shaft to feel its hardness. Her finger slid over the ridge of a vein and toward the swollen head.

"Lay down," she said.

He did as told upon the chaise. Walking over to the candelabra, she plucked out a candle and held it over him.

"You are to stay still," she instructed before tilting the candle.

The hot wax fell onto his stomach. He sucked in his breath but made no sound. Hovering the candle above his left nipple, she dripped more of the wax onto him. She covered his other nipple with wax. As she waited for the wax to melt, she kissed him hard, forcing her tongue into his mouth, imposing her will upon him. She pulled her lips away when he began to respond to her kiss.

"You are mine, Hephaestus," she whispered near his ear. "Mine to do as I desire."

Moving towards his legs, she pressed his erection level with one hand and poured the wax upon it. His hands clenched, and the chains rattled. Smiling, she returned the candle.

"Thank you, Lady Athena."

"You have done well, Hephaestus," she said. "As a reward, you may taste my cunnie."

Straddling his chest, she lowered herself down upon him. She was already wet there, and he would have much to lick. He ran his tongue along her folds, then closed his mouth about her clit and sucked. Gertie closed her eyes and moaned. It was just the right amount of pressure to make her crave for more. Laying her chest along his body, she took the uncovered part of his shaft into her mouth. Reaching below his shaft, she began to fondle him roughly. She pulled at his sack and squeezed his scrotum. His legs jerked at her touch, but he did not disrupt the rhythm of his tongue darting at her clit.

He was skilled, taking the time to find her most sensitive spots. He licked with precision, and she found it difficult to concentrate on her own task of delaying pleasure. His motions stoked the fire in her belly, and she was tempted to buck her hips against his face, but she did not want to disturb the delight his tongue was swirling in her quim. The yearning between her legs stretched for its desired release.

No.

Jerking herself from the pool of pleasure, she lifted herself away from him.

"Let me finish, my lady," he said.

Her breath haggard, she rose to her feet and looked down at him. Her wetness glistened upon his face.

"It will not take long," he added.

That was precisely why she had to stop.

"You like the taste of cunnie, do you?" she asked.

"Its nectar be more delectable than wine, Lady Athena."

"Do you worship the cunnie, Hephaestus?"

"I prefer it to any church."

His words reminded her of her earlier conversation with Lord Barclay.

"It is a divine thing, Lady Athena," he continued. "Yours is divine. Your swollen nub of pleasure protruding from supple, pink folds called to me. I would have worshiped it with my tongue, my mouth, my nose, my fingers—"

"Your nose?"

A corner of his mouth curled. "Your quim has a luscious scent, Lady Athena. I enjoy using any part of me that is at my disposal, especially as my hands are bound."

Gertie curled her toes inside her boot. Her insides churned with curiosity. Her body wanted more of his touch.

"How do you like to spend, Hephaestus?"

"Wrapped inside the chapel of your desire," he quipped.

She picked up her riding crop and let it touch against his inside thigh.

"Lady Athena," he added.

She peeled off the wax that had hardened upon his shaft and obtained from her table a small vial. She poured the contents into her hand, then rubbed the slick salve onto his erection. The liquid seemed to warm against his flesh. She smoothed her hands along his length. He shuddered when her palm swept over the swollen head of his member. His control made her womanhood pulse. Most men she observed had not the fortitude.

Reaching for the candle, she poured another measure of the hot wax just below his navel, perilously close to the tip of his rod. Her other hand wrapped itself tightly about his shaft.

Her hands slid over his length, coaxing the heat churning within his groin. He tried to quell the rising desire.

"Would you like to spend, my Hephaestus?"

"Yes," he said drily.

"Do you feel that you deserve to spend?"

"Not till my lady has spent."

She studied him carefully, then began to tug at his rod more forcefully as she dripped the candle upon his thighs. Tossing the candle away, she straddled his hips and pressed her quim onto the base of his shaft. Rocking her hips, she glided herself along his length. Her wetness there eased the motions. The nearness of her most prized flesh to his member made him breath in sharply. He closed his eyes to regain command.

"Do you hope to ravish me, Hephaestus?"

He opened his eyes to stare at her. God, yes.

"And see how close you are," she said as she teased him by sweeping her flesh close to the head of his shaft, but she would allow no penetration. "Do you imagine how I would feel?"

Again he closed his eyes. He was imagining how her inner folds would feel against him. He imagined the heat of being inside her.

"Would it feel hot and wet? Would you enjoy it?"

He attempted to shut out her words.

"Would you take me hard?"

She ground herself against him. His desire was at the boiling point. He could not stop himself from the thought of pushing her up against the wall and taking her from behind.

"However my lady wishes to be ravished," he said earnestly.

But before he realized it, she had pushed herself off of him. She encased his member in her mouth and sucked hard. Her words, coupled with the sensation bursting upon his shaft, made the dam falter. She took her mouth off him in time for him to shoot his seed all over himself. His climax wracked his entire body, sending tremors through his legs. When at last he felt himself settling back to earth, he saw her smile in triumph.

CHAPTER EIGHT

"I BELIEVE SHE THINKS me your wife—or your mistress," Georgina said with a shudder.

Phineas looked through his quizzing glass at the raven-haired beauty standing next to the statue of Handel on the South Grand Walk at Vauxhall. Her frown as she gazed upon Georgina became a demure smile as she turned her attention to him.

"Yes, I think she would have more sympathy if she knew your true relation to me," Phineas replied as he admired the woman's slender sloping shoulders.

"She's very beautiful," Georgina sniffed. "I think she would satisfy your predilections."

"All women of beauty satisfy me."

Phineas watched as the raven took the arm of a redcoat likely to be her husband. They passed out of the South Walk and into the hall.

"It is a relief to have you back, Phineas. Robert—or his wife, rather—can be exceedingly tiresome. She would have him disavow us as his family."

"Doubtless he would be better situated if he did. We are none of us an asset—you, Abigail, and I."

Georgina sighed. "Am I so terrible because I married in error?"

He patted her hand. "Not at all. I ought be grateful that some of the disdain towards me has been averted by your *crim con*."

"They may disdain me all they wish," she replied with a scowl. "I am tired of hiding from their contemptuous gazes. I suppose they envy me my affair. Those tied to their ugly, wizened husbands abhor that I have found a man who holds me in as much affection and admiration as I him. They loathe that I shall soon be a free woman while they are imprisoned in their miserable marriages."

"Is this man someone you shall find happiness with, m'dear?"

"As soon as Parliament approves the divorce, we shall wed."

"From one marriage into another, Georgina?"

"I have not your aversion to the institution. Shall you never marry, Phineas?"

He wondered, as he studied the middle of the Barclay sisters, if her quick diversion of topic reflected a slight lack of confidence on her part. He would not pursue the matter tonight but determined to himself that he would learn more of this paramour of hers.

"Marriage is a useless institution for me."

"Have you no wish for an heir?"

"Robert is the one who must need worry of an heir. I am still a dead man."

"I think we come across your admirer once more," Georgina remarked as they entered into the hall where the paintings of Thomas Gainsborough hung. "And she appears to be sans her husband."

Phineas discerned the raven to be about four and twenty years of age, married for what he believed to be a short period. She stared blatantly at him with cool blue eyes.

"I will amuse myself with the paintings," Georgina sighed, "that you may have a word with her."

He inclined his head. "You know me too well, m'dear."

After Georgina left his side, he made his way to the raven. In her gown of crystal blue and diamond chandelier earrings, she shined bright in the dim lighting in the hall. The exhilaration of the sport simmered rather than flared in his veins, but he approached her almost by habit.

"How unwise of your husband to leave such a vision to fend for herself," he remarked when he came upon her.

Her bosom with its two orbs pertly pushed above her bodices heaved at his audacity, but she chose to simply correct him. "That was not husband but Sergeant Ames, a friend of the family. My husband is Major Summers, aide-de-camp to the Duke of York."

"And he is unwise to have left you," Phineas reiterated.

"His service often calls him from my side."

She flashed him an alluring smile.

"If I were your husband, I should have left you in more diligent hands than this Sergeant Ames."

"I sent him away to fetch me a glass of lemonade."

The minx. Phineas smiled. "I knew that you were a woman I could appreciate."

"Tell me how it is that I have not seen you here before?"

Phineas looked over at Georgina, who was being rebuffed in her attempts to find a place to sit. One woman had an empty spot next to her but quickly covered the area as Georgina approached. Another couple had turned the other direction upon seeing her.

"You are new to London," he appraised of the raven.

"Yes, this is my first season in town, but I am often here at Vauxhall. The lights here are wondrous, and the entertainment beyond the pale."

She spoke of her favorite performers and was describing the singer set to perform tonight when Phineas spotted the Countess of Lowry. She stood beneath one of the archways with Alexander, who scowled something at her before leaving her side. She wore a silk gown lined with ribbons and lace trim about the neckline, covering what he considered to be a most pleasing bosom. Her feathered headdress did not quite match her gown, but somehow he found her more appealing than usual.

"And I am quite excited to see the balloon ascension," the raven was saying.

Phineas noted Georgina had secured a bench all to herself. She sat staring at the portraiture. He decided he would conclude his *tête-à-tête* with the raven and return to Georgina, but to his surprise, he saw that Lady Lowry had taken a seat next to his sister. Lady Lowry spoke first, Georgina answered, and the two began a conversation.

"Oh dear," the raven groaned, "I think Sergeant Ames has accomplished his task."

A young man in scarlet uniform was indeed approaching them.

"Phillipa Summers," the raven said. "I think I know not your name?"

"Phineas Barclay," he replied with a bow over her hand.

He took his leave before the redcoat reached them. With the entry of the Countess, he had lost interest in the raven. If he were to be assured of arriving at Madame Botreaux's in timely fashion, he would need to depart Vauxhall in twenty minutes. He had no wish to disappoint Lady Athena—not when he had victory in his sights. But the arrival of Lady Lowry was too tempting.

He made his way towards the Countess.

* * * * *

Gertie went to sit beside Mrs. Georgina Westmoreland. Perhaps because Alexander told her that she should shun the woman and Gertie had no desire to accommodate her husband. Since returning from her evening with Hephaestus, she had felt giddy, daring, almost fearless. Over and over her body had relived the delicious sensations he had evoked. She had not wanted to pull away, but what she had done was wrong. Never before had she been so forward, so devilish. But Hephaestus evoked qualities she would never have guessed to have presided within her. She had wanted to spend, desperately. But spending would be the ultimate act of infidelity.

But you were not the first to break the wedding vows, a small voice reasoned.

When Gertie looked upon Mrs. Westmoreland, there was empathy for a woman who perhaps felt trapped in a joyless marriage. She had not seen anyone receive such coldness from others and noted the woman had such sadness in her eyes despite her defiantly lifted chin.

"The pastoral scene is one of my favorite works by Gainsborough," Gertie remarked as she looked at the painting alongside Mrs. Westmoreland.

"Mine as well," Mrs. Westmoreland replied. "I find his paintings possess many facades. One could study it for hours."

Gertie only nodded. Although she appreciated the art, she could not fathom having the patience to stare at it for above a few minutes. Instead, she looked about the hall and glimpsed Lord Barclay talking to a beauty in an ice blue gown. A flush of jealousy crept up her neck. Of course he was engaged in his next conquest. Why should that surprise her?

She had not intended to come this night and much preferred the prospect of being with Hephaestus. Indeed, she welcomed an evening at the *Ballroom* with him. But the Dowager Lowry had expressed a headache, and Gertie did not relish having to spend the evening with Belinda. Sarah, no doubt with similar dread towards having to keep her mother's company, had also opted for Vauxhall. No sooner had brother and sister set foot in the boat when they began arguing over Sarah's marital prospects. Alexander was quite set on an older gentleman by the name of Mr. Rowland and admonished Sarah for not encouraging the man. After pouring out all the reasons why Mr. Rowland would not make a suitable match, Sarah had looked ready to cry. Gertie had begun to sympathize with her sister-in-law. At least her own unhappy marriage had been of her own making.

"They have works by Reynolds at Ranalegh," Gertie said to Mrs. Westmoreland.

"How delightful. I have not been to Ranalegh in some time."

"Nor I."

"I grow weary of London at times."

"And I," sighed Gertie. She liked the lands of Lowry, but Alexander preferred to spend his time in town.

"But it is nice to have found a kindred spirit, if I may be forward. You and I have not conversed much in the past, Countess."

Gertie smiled in empathy. "Perhaps we shall have more occasion hence."

From the corner of her eye, she noticed movement. Lord Barclay was approaching them. Instinctively she sprang to her feet. "I think I shall find my husband and see if he intends to take supper."

Georgina looked at her in surprise but nodded. Gertie took her leave and began to walk briskly towards the maze in the gardens. It was childish of her to avoid Barclay, silly for her to be jealous of the woman he spoke with, and absurd of her to feel any sentiment towards the man. How much easier it was to detest him! Perhaps she still could—she had only to imagine him with Sarah. Their sort deserved each other. Men like him could never appreciate any other kind of woman.

Although the image of him with Sarah fueled her anger, it also made her miserable. She barreled into the maze, upset that she had felt the need to lie to Georgina about going in search of Alexander.

Perhaps she had been better to stay at home with the Dowager. Once Belinda had taken to bed, she could have slipped out and made her way to *Madame Botreaux's*. Now she was all alone in a garden meant for lovers while her husband gallivanted publicly with his mistress.

She walked into a dead-end. Huffing to herself, she turned around and slammed into the body of Lord Barclay. A flush flared through her as she realized who it was. She wanted to demand why the bloody hell he found it necessary to approach her with such proximity, but his hands upon her as he steadied her had her too flustered. She could not recall ever being so firmly grasped by a man. His touch seared straight into her bones and somewhere deep within her.

Satisfied that she had come to no harm, he released her. She took a step from him to gain her composure. She expected him to retreat and allow her passage, but he stood where he was, blocking her exit.

"Sarah—Lady Sarah is not with me," she informed him as she pushed her headdress back in place, hating that she could not keep out the hint of jealousy.

"How fortunate," he replied. "I had hoped to speak with you, Countess."

"Me? Why?"

The words had slipped inelegantly from her in her surprise, but he appeared genuinely stumped by her query for he only stared in response.

Unable to remain silent beneath such study, she assisted him by saying, "You had some matter you sought my audience to address?"

"Yes," he said carefully. "A matter of business, but I will not disturb you here—"

"Are you afeared to broach the matter? Is it quite loathsome?"

He appeared to assess her aggression, no doubt wondering at her antagonism.

"Not at all, Lady Lowry," he said. "Quite the contrary. I have a proposition that could prove beneficial to both parties."

She raised an eyebrow, impatient for their *tête-à-tête* to end.

"The foreman for our copper mine believes there to be significant lode on what could prove Lowry land. We seek access to your properties and would grant you a share of the profits from the copper hauled from that effort."

It was not what she had expected Lord Barclay to present.

"Have you spoken with our steward?" she asked.

"He has but without much progress."

That did not surprise her. The Lowry steward could be quite stubborn in his prejudice of the Barclays.

"And why has the Baron not approached me?"

"Do you wish the truth?"

Gertie blinked. Why would she not?

Taking her silence as an affirmative response, he answered, "My brother thinks that I would present a more persuasive case, though I asserted to him that you abhorred me no small amount."

She would not dispute that. Nonetheless, his honesty and perception thawed a little of her resistance.

"How much of the profit?" she asked.

"Given that we would undertake all the risk and the work, I think ten percent to be fair."

"You would have no profit to share if we did not grant you access."

"Fifteen, then."

Gertrude contemplated the proposal. A partnership between the Farringtons and Barclays would be unheard of, but it would make no sense not to. She could convince their steward of the wisdom of the opportunity. Even Alexander might swallow his reluctance if he could be assured of having more finances to sustain his gambling—or his mistress.

But could she trust the Barclays? Aside from the Farrington family objection to them, she had no reason to distrust the Baron Barclay. As for Phineas…strangely, despite her disapproval of his philandering, she felt a sense of comfort in the way he dealt with her on this matter. She wondered if perhaps his visits with her to the asylum was a means of currying her favor, but if he meant to play the sycophant, he was not very adept at it. No sooner had he become more favorable in her view, he was sure to utter something that riled her like no other.

Yet how could she trust a rakehell? A man who had engaged in a duel and *killed*.

"I had asked my brother to assume the negotiations," Barclay said, as if reading her mind, "for he has not my tarnished reputation, but he is not partial to such dealings."

She wanted more space to think, but she knew the proposition to hold minimal risk for Lowry or the family.

"I have no wish for you to shoulder all the risk and all the work," she pronounced. "We have tenants who have little means of income. If we grant you access, I wish for your mine to employ some of our men."

"That will cut into the profit for all of us."

She nodded. "I understand."

He studied her, perhaps wondering what sort of woman he was dealing with and if she had a sound mind for business.

"Done. I will have Mr. Hancock draw up the details with your steward."

She nodded. "I appreciate your seeking our consent for you could have easily dug beneath our lands without our knowledge."

"We Barclays are not always as loathsome as the Farringtons would wish to believe." He paused and once again fixed his stare upon her. "But you are not like the other Farringtons."

Her heart hammered beneath her bosom at the intensity of his gaze. Why did it feel as if he meant to probe the recesses of her soul?

"What—what do you mean by such a statement?" she stammered, though she believed that he meant her a form of compliment.

"How does a person with your compassion and your qualities become a Farrington?"

His question prompted her defenses. Lacking an answer that she was willing to share with the likes of him, she turned to the only reservoir she felt comfortable drawing upon at the moment: her jealousy.

"Certainly you do not intend to demean a Farrington, Lord Barclay? I know you to be quite partial to at least one Farrington…"

Her response did not have the benefit she had desired for her own sake. Instead of feeling in a position of command, she felt weak and trifling. She made a move to walk by him, but he did not budge.

"Mine is a sport your tender persuasion would not understand."

"And I am glad for it!"

This time she brushed past him, not caring that she had to collide with his left side. She did not look back to see his expression. She only knew she had to escape his presence before she lost control of her nerves and smacked him across the face or, worse, began to cry in front of him.

* * * * *

Phineas watched as the Countess headed in a direction that would take her further into the maze. He had apparently done much to offend her, but her vehemence startled him. Had he not flattered her with his remarks? Or did Alexander and his family yet manage to command a form of loyalty from her? He shook his head, refusing to believe it. None of the Farringtons deserved such devotion. He had seen the way Alexander spoke to his wife and the sneer upon the Dowager when she looked upon Gertrude—er, Lady Lowry. Sarah could not disparage her sister-in-law enough—he doubted her ability to coat her animosity.

All that notwithstanding, he did not believe the Countess to be a dolt despite her occasional awkwardness—which, as he spent more time in her company, he found rather delightful. She was a woman of obvious intelligence. That she would marry into the family could simply have been the allure of title and prestige, of ignorance upon her part as to the true nature of the Farringtons, or even misguided affection for Alexander, who had both countenance and the ability to charm when he so desired. As Mrs. Pemberly had alluded, the Farringtons were unworthy of Gertrude. But why such sensitivity when he broached the subject of her husband and in-laws?

He had detected a note of jealousy in her words, but that did not surprise him. The Countess was plain and her sister-in-law beautiful. But perhaps her jealousy stemmed from more than mere envy of Sarah's attributes? He recalled how her breath had left her when he had helped her off her horse. That small respiratory pause was barely perceptible, but he was too skilled in the art of seduction not to have noticed. That awareness had enlivened him in a way he had not expected.

Glancing at the position of the moon, he realized he would have to depart soon if he were to make it to the *Ballroom*. He was confident that if he kept Lady Athena waiting, she would be done with him. All his efforts would be for naught, and he had every intention of conquering her. But if he left, he would be leaving the Countess to wander in the maze when he could easily direct her out. He had had too many trysts in this wonderful garden not to know his way around.

He walked over to a marble statue and waited. The Countess would eventually realize her error and retrace her steps.

As he predicted, the Countess emerged, but upon seeing him, she quickly turned to her right and headed down another row that would lead her nowhere. A minute later, she returned. Refusing to make eye contact, she strode past him and headed in the other direction.

"That path takes you to a pretty little fountain," he informed her.

She halted in her steps. He suspected she was grinding her teeth. She whirled around to face him.

"Why are you here, Lord Barclay?"

"To make myself available should you require my assistance."

She bristled.

He took a step towards her. She had better accept his aid with gratitude for he was about to ruin his prospects with Lady Athena.

"A debaucher with *noblesse oblige*?" she asked. "Your services are unnecessary. I am content to—"

"Wander aimlessly and admire the shrubbery?"

"A far better way to pass the time than in your company!"

She walked in the correct direction. He followed. They reached a fork in the path, and she chose the wrong one yet again. She had as much sense for direction as she did for fashion, he decided.

Suddenly she stopped in her tracks. She stood frozen for a moment before spinning on her heels, brushing by him with all speed. He saw a look of dismay upon her. Turning his head to see what had prompted her vexation, he saw Alexander, his face buried in the neck of a brunette. If the Countess had not known of Alexander's mistress, she knew it now.

Phineas hurried after Lady Lowry.

"Countess—"

He silently cursed Alexander for a bastard.

"Countess," he tried again as she barreled down another misleading path. "Lady Low—"

Turning around, she demanded, "Why do you persist in following me?"

He gazed deep into her eyes and saw that she had known of Alexander's infidelity. He marveled a little at her fortitude.

"*Noblesse oblige*," he offered.

"Sir, you may take your bloody *noblesse oblige* and shove it up your arse!"

He stared at her. Her language surprised even herself for she began to blush. He was about to commit a horrible mistake, one that could destroy the agreement they had come to earlier over the mine and give Robert several more hairs of gray, one that would make permanent her loathing of him. But her show of defiance was too irresistible. She had spoken with such command, such unabashed ardor...

Grabbing her by the arm, he pulled her to him and brought his lips down upon hers as he wrapped his other hand behind her head. Stunned, she allowed him to kiss her. He pressed his mouth firmly upon her soft, plump lips. And then she gave way. He found himself sinking into her mouth, his tongue brushing hers. She tasted divine. The warm wetness of her mouth mixed with the feel of her body so close to him made the blood course forcefully in his veins and pound in his head. With his hand still upon her head, he angled her in the different ways he wished to devour her. Whole mouthfuls were not enough. He desired to have her body pinned against him.

Just when he suspected she meant to return his kiss, she tore away. Surprised, he let her go. She had stumbled a few steps away from him and stood staring at him, a few tendrils of hair loosened near her nape and her rouge mussed along the lines of her lips. She looked beautiful.

He could not tell if she was angry. Flustered, yes. With any other woman he would have smiled, confident of his effect upon her, or he would have advanced, a predator coming upon its doomed prey. But he did neither. He waited to see how the Countess would react and what she would say.

Lady Lowry hesitated, as if wanting to speak, but wordlessly she turned away from him, and despite her addled state, ventured down the path that took her out of the maze and away from him.

CHAPTER NINE

WHY HAD HE KISSED her? Gertie wondered as she pulled out a diaphanous chemise to wear to Madame Botreaux's later that evening. It had been two days since Vauxhall, and yet her body flushed with the memory as if it had been but an hour ago. Over and over she recalled how masterfully his mouth had moved over hers, how fully he took her in. Her jaw had never been worked with such vigor. Her body felt ignited and weak all at once. She had never thought a mere kiss could be so involved, so engaging, so thrilling. Little wonder women overlooked his faults. His kiss had the ability to wash away their discretion.

Indeed, she had forgotten where she was, even who she was. She was aware only of him and his effect upon her. The warmth of his nearness, the pressure of his hand upon her head—how secure and comforting that had felt, the heat of his mouth, the surge of longing in her loins. She wanted the kiss should never end. How she had summoned the will to break away from him, she knew not. With relief she had made her way out of the maze. Her heart had fluttered with the ferocity of a butterfly's wings. She could focus on nothing thereafter—not the food, nor the music, not the daring acrobats who made the audience gasp as they flipped and somersaulted over one another high above the heads. How she envied Sarah, who would have had no qualms in surrendering her body to Barclay.

Had he kissed her to prove he could? Gertie wondered. Did he think it some reward for her acquiescence to the mine? Or had he acted out of pity? Her cheeks burned at the thought. Barclay might have seen Alexander with his mistress. Perhaps Barclay intended to provide her a set-down for her rudeness. And she had given him the satisfaction that she did not object to his kiss for she could not muster a word in response. Instead of pushing him away the instant she knew what he was about to do, she had given in, had surrendered to his lips and allowed this tongue to probe where none other had. And enjoyed every moment.

Gertie shook her head. She had had every intention of visiting the *Ballroom* that evening, but she did not. Instead, she had sat down to write a letter to Harrietta, divulging all that had occurred between her and Lord Barclay, only to tear the letter, begin anew, and toss it aside. Over and over.

In her latest correspondence, the Marchioness had invited Gertrude for a stay at Dunnesford. Gertie decided she would accept the invitation.

> *Dearest Hettie,*
>
> *With much joy, I welcome your invitation to stay at Dunnesford. I have missed your friendship dearly and can hardly wait to greet the little one. He is sure to be as handsome as his mother. I have much to share with you and admit to being beside myself. Never have I felt such uncertainty and such confusion. I am not myself. I regret that I shall leave you in suspense, but I cannot find the proper words to describe it all.*
>
> *My regards to the Marquess and to your family.*
>
> *Humbly and faithfully,*
> *Gertie*

Settling upon her Grecian gown and sandals, Gertie prepared herself for *Madame Botreaux's*.

* * * * *

I am not myself, Phineas thought to himself after he had walked into the wrong alcove and nearly tripped over a couple who lay prostrate upon the ground, writhing in pleasure.

"How fortunate you are that Lady Athena chose not to come that night you were absent," Lance had commented last night. "Penelope and I were convinced that you would fail with her. Lady

Athena would have been furious to discover your absence, but you have the devil's luck, Barclay."

Phineas knew he had risked an end to his liaison with Lady Athena, but he couldn't tear himself from Vauxhall. After escaping the maze, the Countess had managed to elude him the rest of the evening. He wanted a word with her. He wanted to know how she felt about the kiss. He wanted to ask her pardon if that was warranted. Those who knew him well would have it considered it outlandish that Phineas Barclay should ever entertain the notion of apologizing for a kiss, but the thought of having the Countess irate—truly irate—not the exasperation he knew he had provoked in the past—gnawed at him.

But Lady Luck had not favored him in that respect for despite his best attempts, he could not get near the Countess. He had opportunity to study her from afar during the performance of the acrobats, but he could discern no emotion from her. Instead, his staring caught the attention of Sarah, who thought she was the purpose of his attentions and not her sister-in-law, who sat beside her. After the entertainment, he had made his way towards Gertrude. If he would have to engage in conversation with Sarah in order to gain access to Lady Lowry, so be it. But his path was blocked by Phillipa Summers.

"A pleasure to have made your acquaintance, sir," she said, holding out her hand.

He took it and kissed it ceremoniously. When he released her, he discovered a note in his palm. He smiled to hide his irritation. The Countess was now joined by Alexander and the trio were making their way towards the exit.

"My dear, you are not thinking of seducing Lady Sarah?" Georgina had commented as he saw her to her new townhome.

Feigning a yawn, he had replied, "It was an accomplishment of vast uninterest."

Georgina frowned. "Oh, Phineas. Of all the wretched creatures to…why?"

He waved his quizzing glass. "Why not? She is not as distasteful as you would believe."

"She may be beautiful, but I am convinced she is every bit as odious as I would believe. If you have done with her, why were you staring at her all evening?"

He paused. He had no wish to tell a falsehood but he was not ready to explain anything to Georgina.

But a woman's intuition won out nonetheless.

"The Countess. You were staring at the Countess!"

"What a strange observation, Georgina."

"I saw you go after her in the garden. Is your intention to seduce the whole clan of Farringtons?"

"I had a business proposition with the Countess."

Georgina looked skeptical.

"Have I ever lied to you?" he challenged.

"No, but neither are you always forthcoming with the truth."

Smiling, he kissed her forehead. "Good night, Georgina."

He could tell she did not want an end to their dialogue, but she knew better than to goad him.

"She is not like the Farringtons," Georgina said.

"So I've been told."

"And she is no Miss Summers."

"Definitely not."

She pouted her lips at his irritating concurrence.

"M'dear, if I knew not better, I'd vouch you had developed some affection for the Countess," Phineas remarked, making Georgina the subject.

"She was kind to me," Georgina defended.

"Perhaps she lacks discretion."

"Are you suggesting she ought not have spoken with me?"

"Consorting with you does not improve one's reputation, does it? Now, as you are my sister, I am obligated to…"

After emitting an indignant gasp, Georgina whirled on her heels and left him standing on the threshold alone. He let out a breath of relief. He had no wish to discuss the Countess further with Georgina. Not until he had more lucidity of his own.

* * * * *

Lady Athena had him kneel before her once more. Phineas suspected she did not like her men to tower above her. She pushed her breasts into his face and commanded him to suckle her teats. He readily complied. There was an odd energy in Lady Athena tonight, almost an urgency, but he felt ready to take advantage of it. As he fit as much of one fleshy orb as he could into his mouth, he sensed her eyes closed behind her mask. Her body had relaxed, allowing him to guide the motions. Tonight was the night. He would win Lady Athena at last.

Her costume was unusual, though fitting to her nom de plume. In her layers of translucent linen, she appeared almost virginal but for the golden mask and helmet. He liked the way the straps of her sandals wound around her lower leg. Lady Athena could wear almost anything, and he would find it enticing. If he could coax her out of her garments, he would have attained no small victory. Her attire was a source of power for her.

He sensed her desire building as he nipped and sucked a nipple. She let out a low moan and arched her bosom into his face. Gently, he placed his hands upon her hips to aid in her balance. He increased the vigor of his suckling to distract her from his right hand, which he drifted down her thigh as his fingers began to collect the thin fabric separating him from her flesh. When he had pulled up the hem to her thigh, he slipped his hand beneath the chiton.

Her own hands were wound through his hair. She grasped him tightly whenever he sucked with too much vehemence. He reached his thumb between her thighs and slid it between the folds to connect with the nub of flesh there. Slowly he circled his thumb against her pliant flesh. Suppressing his own urges, he focused on teasing the now swollen nub with light strokes. She lifted a leg and placed her foot upon the stool next to him, allowing him better access to the forbidden treasure. Victory was indeed in sight.

He could smell her desire, feel it coating his thumb as he slid the digit against her, graduating from tender caresses to a more aggravated fondling. Her body quivered at his ministrations. Her breath grew uneven. He brushed his thumb rapidly across her clit. Lady Athena was a slow burning furnace—perhaps from a lack of frequent *orgasmos*. Her desire built steadily but slowly. Nonetheless, he would sooner die from exhaustion before she reached her climax. And hers was nearing. He could tell from the straining of her body and the uncontrollable gasps escaping her lips.

Suddenly she had her hands upon his shoulders and shoved him away. She stumbled back and took in a deep but haggard breath. Startled, he wondered if perhaps she had spent without him knowing. He knew many women who achieved small climaxes, sometimes in advance of a grand climax. But Lady Athena did not have the look of a woman satisfied.

After she had collected her breath, she straightened herself.

"You are not without skill, Hephaestus," she said with a slight tremor despite her best attempts to appear regal. "But we are done."

"Done for the evening, Lady Athena?" he inquired.

She shook her head. "Done."

The finality in her tone needed no further clarification. Taking up her riding crop, she strode out of the alcove without further word.

"Ah, Phineas, you are even better than your repute," sighed Penelope as she collapsed into her bed an hour later.

Still hard, he lay beside the proprietress and gazed at the canopy above her bed.

"She didn't say a word," he murmured as he stroked his hardness. His thoughts of Lady Athena had not left him once as Penelope collected upon her wager. She was not the sort to inspire desire in him, but fortunately, one of his talents lay in his ability to command an erection whenever needed.

"Were you expecting an adieu of some kind?" Penelope asked.

"She was near to spending," he said.

"Are you sure? It is not always easy to know with a woman."

"I know," he disputed. "It was as if she feared to spend."

"You had her as near to it as anyone from what I saw." Her hand wandered between her legs. "But our Lady Athena is a mystery."

"I have not done with her."

"Sorry to disappoint you, *mon cheri*, but Lady Athena has never been known to alter her mind."

"There is always a way."

"I would be happy to put up another wager," Penelope murmured as she fondled herself more intently.

Unlike Lady Athena, Penelope did not take long to begin her ascent. Seeing that she was aroused once more, he positioned himself between her spread legs and thrust himself inside of her.

Her cunnie lacked the tightness of bodies less traversed, but her muscles inside were strong, and she used them well against his shaft. Soon she was spasming beneath him as her cries echoed off the walls. He pulled out of her after she had settled into a contented stupor.

Phineas contemplated pleasuring himself till he spent but chose instead to leave his erection unattended and went to collect his garments.

"Come again soon," Penelope murmured.

Phineas said nothing. He had received a note from Phillipa indicating she would be spending some time at her sister's outside of London, but that her sister would not be at home, leaving her alone and in want of company. He decided he would relieve Miss Summers of her loneliness.

CHAPTER TEN

THE DRIVER OF THE post-chaise had given Gertie a skeptical look when he realized she was traveling sans an abigail but seemed somewhat appeased when she named her destination, figuring there was ample pay to be had. Lowry House could not spare a maid for her trip to Dunnesford, and Gertie preferred to be alone. The weather seemed to know her mood and matched it with grey skies and drops of rain.

Sarah had seemed out of sorts the past few days as well, Gertie recalled. Her sister-in-law was crosser than usual and seemed to turn a frequent and suspicious eye towards her. Gertie had no desire to speculate what she had done this time to merit Sarah's hostility and had kept her head down as if she was not aware of Sarah's scrutiny.

"Have you heard from Lord Barclay?" Sarah had finally asked after aimlessly viewing the latest edition of *The Lady's Magazine*.

"Wh-why should I have heard from Lord Barclay?" Gertie had responded. She had not even ventured to visit the orphan asylum for fear of running into the man.

The Dowager raised an eyebrow from the sofa where she sat with her embroidery.

"I ask because you were seen in his company."

"He—he insisted on escorting me home," Gertie replied, hoping Sarah was not referring to that night at Vauxhall.

"Why are we discussing that man?" Belinda inquired.

"I heard the servants say that he has sent many a correspondence to Gertie," Sarah offered.

But I have not lifted my skirts beneath him, Gertie thought to herself.

Belinda turned her disapproving eye upon Gertie. "Why are you corresponding with such a man?"

"It was my refusal to grant him an audience that prompted him to write me so often," Gertie explained. "The Barclays wished to confer upon our properties."

Belinda snorted. "We will have nothing to do with that horrid family. They are a menace to polite society."

Not able to obtain the intelligence she desired, Sarah became even more irritable. Only Alexander had seemed to be in good spirits, having secured an offer for Sarah's hand from Mr. Rowland. Sarah had burst into tears at the announcement, but when Gertie attempted to console her, she had bared her fangs and thrust Gertie aside.

The rain came down in heavy sheets. The chaise lumbered awkwardly through the mud. It would take thrice as long to reach Dunnesford in these conditions. Gertie wondered if her portmanteau would survive the rain for she could not remember the driver covering her belongings. She heard the man curse as one side of the carriage sunk into the mud. The driver cracked the whip above the horses, but the mud clung tenaciously to the chaise. Gertie shook her head. Fate was having no pity upon her.

The whip cracked once more. This time the chaise lurched forward but without one of its wheels. The vehicle tipped towards its side, tumbling Gertie into the window. The driver let out a string of oaths. Shaking off the knock to her head, Gertie managed to climb out the carriage door and into the pouring rain. Her feet disappeared into the mud as she stepped off the carriage. She pulled her cloak tighter about her shoulders, a fruitless endeavor for the mud was seeping into her petticoats from below.

"Lost 'er wheel," the driver told her, stating the obvious.

"What can I do to help?" she asked.

"If I holds the chaise, yer ken slip the wheel on."

She nodded and reached for the wheel, realizing afterwards that she should have removed her gloves before reaching into the mud.

The driver grabbed the axel and lifted it as high as he could while Gertie attempted to push the wheel back into place. But the driver could not lift the carriage high enough. Nor could Gertie lift the large and heavy wheel. In her attempt to do so, she landed herself in the mud. She wiped the splatter from her face with her sleeve.

"Thar be an inn not half a league from 'ere," the driver informed her.

"I take it you'll be needing assistance," a voice from the rain said.

A shiver went through her bones at the sound. Impossible, she told herself, but when she turned, despite the rain clinging to her eyelashes, she saw a bay she recognized. Upon its owner sat Phineas Barclay. As with her, he was sodden from head to toe, but no doubt he did not appear nearly as wretched. His valet, also upon a bay, traveled beside him.

"Good sir," the driver greeted, "could yar man assist us? We've lost 'er wheel."

"Yes, I can see that," Barclay replied. "Francis could lend you a hand, but you'll not travel far on a wheel without its collet and split pin."

The driver looked around him and frowned. He began to wade through the mud in search of the missing parts.

"I should take the lady to the nearest posting inn and will leave you my man Francis."

"We were faring well enough," Gertie replied, then realized the stupidity of her statement.

Barclay raised a skeptical eyebrow.

"Very well," she relented, though she preferred to brave the rains with her driver and Francis.

Barclay held out his hand. She put her dirtied glove in his and allowed him to hoist her onto his horse before him. She realized her muddied garments would soil his finer clothes, but he should not have offered to take her if he worried of the effect. It was damnably uncomfortable riding side saddle with a man already upon the horse. Even worse that the man should be Lord Barclay. She could not position her body in such a way to avoid having her rump from fitting against his crotch—and when she tried, she nearly fell off the horse.

"Perhaps it would be best if one of us walked," she suggested after he had caught her by the waist to keep her from slipping off.

"You would have us tarry longer in the rain?" he returned.

Gertrude pressed her lips together. There was naught to say unless she wished to reveal how uncomfortable he made her feel.

Barclay urged his horse into a cantor. The movement caused

her to bump into him incessantly. At one point the wet and sagging feathers of her bonnet caught him the mouth.

"How coincidental that you should have happened upon us," she said to distract herself from the jostling of her body against his. "One would think you were following me, Lord Barclay."

"I am visiting a friend in Hampton. And what has put you on this wet and rainy path, Lady Lowry?"

"I, too, am visiting a friend—the Marchioness of Dunnesford."

She longed to ask why he had kissed her that night at Vauxhall, but he behaved as if it had not happened. Perhaps it had been an impulsive act and one that he regretted. If he had sooner forgotten what had happened, she should have no wish to bring up the matter. She resorted to a safe subject—the weather.

"Do you suppose the rain will let up soon?" she asked.

"Hard to predict. If it does not, we shall be much delayed to our respective destinations. The roads will not be traversable."

She frowned at the prospect. When they reached the Four Horse Posting Inn, a modest two storied building with a thatched roof, the rain seemed to be coming down even harder. Barclay assisted her off his horse. With her skirts sodden down into the very last petticoat, Gertrude felt as if she were dragging along something twice her weight.

"A room for my lady and an abigail to assist her," Barclay informed the innkeeper.

"Come, my lady, we shall put your things up by the fire, shall we?" said the innkeeper's wife, Mrs. Pettigrew. She had a ruddy but cheerful face.

Gertrude removed her bonnet and cloak, which Mrs. Pettigrew hung before a blazing fire.

"You best shed your garments afore you catch a chill," Mrs. Pettigrew commented.

"My articles are with the chaise, and perhaps no drier than I am," Gertie said. "I shall sit by the fire and dry myself."

Not long after the driver and Barclay's valet arrived at the inn. The wheel had been fixed, but the roads were in no condition for travel.

Gertie went through her trunk in her small but tidy room upstairs. To her relief, not all her articles were soaked in rain. She found a dry pair of stockings, her high-necked chemise, corset, and a gown of blue with long sleeves and a wide sash of gold.

"You could borrow a few of my petticoats," Mrs. Pettigrew offered.

The innkeeper's wife was shorter and stouter, but Gertie welcomed the opportunity to step out of her sodden apparel. Mrs. Pettigrew had one of her scullery maids wash the mud-stained gown, stockings, and shoes.

"Thank you. You have been most kind," Gertie said when she had donned her new attire.

"Such beautiful thick tresses you have," Mrs. Pettigrew said. "Alas, I've not much skill in dressing."

Mrs. Pettigrew had attempted to pin all of Gertie's wet hair atop her head, but the heavy hair would not stay in place easily and leaned lopsided to one side of her head.

Mr. Pettigrew knocked on the door. "Your husband awaits in the parlor and asks if you will join him in a meal?"

"He's not my hus–" Gertie began, then wondered at the propriety of her traveling alone and having arrived with a man not her husband.

"I made a pigeon pie—fresh baked this morning," Mrs. Pettigrew said.

Gertie considered her hunger and decided to go downstairs. The innkeeper had set a nice table with Mrs. Pettigrew's meat pie, bread, cheese, potatoes with butter, and stewed apples.

Lord Barclay stood before an inviting fireplace. Like her, he had changed into drier clothes. His wet hair had been pulled back and tied at the neck with a black ribbon. His dark blue waistcoat was astonishingly simple considering its owner, but as always, he wore it well over his linen of billowing sleeves. She glimpsed him in deep thought and felt a surprising tenderness as she admired his profile. Something about the way he looked then made her want to cradle him in her arms. Then her growling stomach caught his attention.

"Ah, Countess," he greeted, approaching her and offering his arm. He seemed genuinely pleased to see her.

She allowed him to lead her to the table and pull a chair for her. After sitting down, he filled her glass.

"To a better journey than we have had," he said as he raised his glass.

Gertie drank to that. The wine was surprisingly smooth, and she took another sip.

"What a delightful inn we have stumbled upon," she said as she dug her fork into Mrs. Pettigrew's pie. "How fortunate we were to have been near it."

"I suppose…" she added, "that I should be grateful for your arrival."

He looked at her over his glass of wine. He sat to the side of his chair, one leg crossed over the other.

"You've no need to thank me, Countess. I suspect I was the last person you desired to see upon the road."

She flushed at the truth of his statement. She reached for the bread and pulled off a large piece. "The circumstances surrounding your arrival were a trifle trying. I think naught but the appearance of the sun should have made me happy. But I thank you for your assistance. Were it not for you and your valet, my driver and I might still be stuck and the chaise unfixed."

He seemed to smile to himself as he took a sip of his wine.

"You find humor in our situation, sir?" she asked.

"Do you always do what you deem you are obligated to do?"

She stopped chewing her bread as if she had tasted a worm. "You speak as if that were a disapproving trait?"

"It is admirable to some extent, but confess: you had no desire to thank me."

She stared at his handsome but aggravating façade and considered the prospect of dining alone in her room, but she was far too hungry to leave the table.

"What does it matter what I desire?" she returned. "You came to our aid, and it is only proper that I thank you for it."

"It always matters what you desire."

She began to butter her bread to avoid having to look into his penetrating stare. It did not matter that her bread had already received one coat of butter.

"How simple for you," she stated. "No doubt in your world men and women should behave on their impulses alone with no regard for courtesy or convention."

"I think you would find it liberating."

"Perhaps I would, but that is no way for polite society to conduct itself."

"You prefer that we swallow the truth of our emotions and feign falsehoods for the sake of convention?"

"That is hardly what I said! I merely stated…"

She saw the glimmer of amusement in his eyes. He was playing with her.

"Would you care for more bread with your butter, Countess?" inquired Barclay.

Gertie glanced down at her bread, now top heavy with coats of butter. She felt her flush deepen and was grateful for the shadows cast by the fireplace. Perhaps he would not notice how much he tested her.

"No, thank you," she replied, taking a bite of her butter, then drenching it away with wine. "I was merely trying to thank you for your service, but if you've no wish for the recognition, I will gladly withdraw my gratitude."

"I never said I did not wish for it. Indeed, for the likes of me to receive thanks from you, Countess, is a rare and special occasion. But when I said that you've no need to thank me, I had hoped to relieve you from an awkward obligation."

"If I am awkward, it is only because of you," she retorted, setting aside her bread permanently in favor of her wine glass. "You hardly make it easy for me, sir. And I've no doubt you behave in such vexing fashion on purpose."

Finishing the contents, she refilled her glass.

"My apologies, Lady Lowry," he said. "It is not my intention to vex you always."

"Now you are the one with pretenses, Lord Barclay. I am convinced it is always your intention to vex me or you would not have…"

He raised his eyebrows, but she could finish her sentence. Instead she took another sip of wine.

"Kissed you?" he finished.

She took another sip to calm her irritation. She had decided it was best to ignore what had happened at Vauxhall, especially when it became clear that they would have to suffer each other's company for some time. It had seemed he might have even forgotten what had happened. But, fool that she was, she had made mention of what happened that night.

"You were wrong to have been so forward," she told him. "I am not my sister-in-law."

"That, my lady, is evident," he responded wryly.

She narrowed her eyes. Did he mean to imply that she was not as pretty as Sarah, or as pleasurable and engaging?

"I have not her loose…disposition," she informed.

"Why not?"

She stared in disbelief. "Why not? Do you ask such a question in earnest?"

"Dead earnest."

Her heartbeat quickened, sensing the impending danger of such dialogue.

"A man of your morals would not understand," she evaded.

"What is there to understand, Countess? Conventions? Courtesies?"

"Yes!" she snapped, finishing the rest of her wine.

He sat back in thought. "What would become of your conventions and courtesies if you indulged in loose…desires?"

"Then we should become a society filled with persons like you!"

"A very distressing thought," he agreed.

She stared at her wine glass, regretting that she had drank her fill so quickly.

"But truth be told," he continued, "you could never become the likes of me—or your sister-in-law—for you've too much courtesy, too much regard for others."

She looked at him in surprise through her haze. Did he mean that as a compliment?

"So I ask once more: why not indulge yourself, Countess?"

"Indulge in what?"

"Anything you wish. Fine clothing, amusement, a paramour of your own…"

"I've no need for such things."

"We all have a need for love. We are creatures of emotion."

Gertie bristled. "And what sort of love do you find in these things? You clothe yourself in fineries and amuse yourself with games of seduction—have *you* found love?"

"No," he said gravely.

She knit her brows. Then why did he…? She was having difficulty following his logic.

"But," he added. "I have not closed myself from the possibility of it, as you have."

"I am *married*," she reminded him.

"And that is your defense? Forgive me if I find it a poor excuse."

Her jaw dropped. "Of course. Matrimony means nothing to a man of your sort."

She wanted to storm away from the table. Her heart was beating faster than before, but she needed a moment to focus, to stop the room from wobbling.

"Have you love in your marriage then?"

"You are impertinent, sir!"

"You did not answer affirmatively."

Her heart pounded painfully against her chest now. She could not take a comfortable breath.

"It is none of your affair," she said and moved her reluctant body to its feet.

"You may deny me the truth, but I hope you do not deny yourself, Countess."

The softness of his tone made tears leap to her eyes. She should not have consumed that wine. Gripping the table, she turned to him.

"For what purpose do you engage in such discussions with me?" she threw at him, trembling with anger. "Why do you persist in—in—asking me questions—in vexing me?"

"Because I pity you."

She stood in stunned silence, then felt a violent urge to scream and toss the bottle of wine at his head.

"Sod off!" she swore. "I've no need for your bloody pity."

"You've a need for it and more, Countess."

"Is that why you kissed me? Because you pitied me?" she cried. The realization filled her with rage and sorrow. To prevent herself from crying, she reached for the bottle of wine, but he was upon his feet, catching her arm in midair. He took the bottle from her with his free hand. She cried out in anguish as she attempted to jerk herself free from his grasp.

"You are the most atrocious…" she spat, desperate to contain the tears that threatened to slip down her face. "I wish I had never set eyes upon you! I wish you had never returned to England!"

"If you allowed yourself half the passion with which you hate and despise me–"

He struggled to make her look at him.

"You know nothing of me or my passion, you arrogant bastard!"

"I know yours is a loveless marriage. I know because Alexander is incapable of love. I know you suffer yourself to be a martyr of some sort, denying yourself the pleasure of love and flesh while your husband treats his mistress with more regard–"

"*Damn you. Damn your insolence!*"

She tore herself successfully from his grasp, but stumbled to the ground from her own exertion. Free of him, the tears began slipping from her eyes.

"Gertie–"

She sensed him kneeling behind her, felt his hand upon her shoulder, but she swung at his arm, catching him on the jaw with the back of her hand. He pressed his lips into a firm line, then reached for the back of her head and pulled her to him, crushing his lips to her mouth. Her body, already warm from the emotions coursing through her, flared like fire.

The kiss felt bruising and punishing. Unlike the kiss at Vauxhall, this one seemed intended to suffocate her. She could not breathe. What little air she could take in through her nostrils was filled with the scent of him. She could not determine if it was the wine that he had imbibed or her own that she tasted. She pushed, pulled, and swatted at him, but her arms might have been the leaves of flowers for all their effectiveness. He held her fast, his mouth cemented to hers. She would have cried out from the pressure had she possession of her own mouth.

And then she surrendered. Surrendered to the fury of emotions raging inside her. Surrendered to the heat and power of him.

She returned his kiss every bit as fiercely. The world about her rocked with the violence of a ship tossed by a stormy sea. Grasping his waistcoat, her knuckles white, she held onto him for dear life. She pulled him to her and pushed her lips up at him. His mouth covered hers as if he meant to swallow her whole. She tasted his lips with the desperation of a wanderer in the desert seeking to extract the last drops of dew. Her body burned with longing, seeking to become one with him through their mouths.

"Would my lord and lady care for—"

Gertie pulled herself from Barclay at the entry of the innkeeper. She scrambled to her feet, her cheeks burning, and stumbled from the room.

CHAPTER ELEVEN

T HE INNKEEPER CLEARED his throat uncomfortably as Lord Barclay's nostrils flared. It was not the fault of the innkeeper, but Phineas could have killed the man. He rose to his feet and sauntered to the table with more calm than he felt.

"Would—would my lord care for some sherry?" Mr. Pettigrew stuttered. "Or a pudding? The missus bakes a mighty fine..."

"No," Phineas replied.

Nodding, the innkeeper scurried away. Alone, Phineas sat down and retrieved his snuffbox. He sighed through his nose. The snuff was a poor substitute for the intoxication of Lady Lowry's lips. After inhaling a dose of the tobacco, he turned to stare into the fire. His body needed time to cool. The blood drained slowly from his engorged shaft.

The Countess had consumed her wine too fast. He could see the glazed look in her eyes and the uncertainty of her movements. He could not know how much of her kiss was the effect of the wine, and he should be glad for the interruption of the innkeeper. Not that he had allowed a woman's drunken state to stop him before, but he suspected Gertie was not practiced in holding her wine, and he would not take advantage of a vulnerability induced by wine.

God help him. He needed no wine. He was consumed by her. Even now, he could feel the softness of her lips upon his own, smell her scent upon him. Deprived of her presence, his body tortured itself with longing.

He would hardly have considered himself a romantic, but the firelight dancing upon her visage, stoking the glow in her eyes, had entranced him. Even the way her wet hair had became undone in the fury of their kiss he found appealing. A single rivulet of water had wound its way from her neck and down over the top of a breast.

He wanted nothing but to crush her body to his, to feel those heavy orbs pressing against his chest.

He could hardly believe his luck when he had come upon her in the rain looking a miserable creature covered in mud. He knew few women who would have braved the dirt to fix the wheel of a carriage in drenching rain. He had shaken his head for once again she traveled without servants. Such a stubborn, self-sacrificing, selfless…admirable woman. He regretted having criticized her riding habit that day they rode back from the orphan asylum. Lady Lowry may have lacked any talent in the realm of fashion, but her attentions were more properly placed than many a fine dressed person. If only she would consider herself a more fitting priority.

Rising to his feet, he picked up the guilty bottle of burgundy and poured himself a glass. He thought about Gertie in her room. What would she think of him when she came to her senses? Might she abhor him more because this time she had returned his kiss? The blood coursed more strongly through him at the memory. His desire to devour her had overcome him. He could not endure her tears—tears that he had caused. He wanted her to surrender to her desires, to stop denying herself passion and happiness. He wanted to stamp out all the misery her marriage and the Farringtons had impressed upon her.

The Countess was capable of much passion. He had suspected it for some time, but the fervor with which she had kissed him tonight confirmed it. She hid that flame deep inside of her, and he wished to unearth it. No woman had ever sparked such curiosity in him, and he would never have guessed to find himself so taken by a woman as outwardly uninspiring as Gertie. There lay a greater mystery in the Countess of Lowry, and he intended to discover it.

* * * * *

Laying with his arms crossed behind his head in bed, Phineas had thought the Countess to be sleeping off the effects of the wine when a knock at his door prompted him from his bed. He pulled on his banyan. Opening the door, he expected to find one of the innkeeper's maids, who had been casting demure smiles at him all evening as she cleared the dining table. He was surprised to see

Gertie, dressed only in her night shift and stays, a flimsy shawl wrapped about her shoulders.

"Lady Lowry, is something wrong?" he inquired.

"I saw a light from your door," she said. "May I—may I come in?"

Surprised by the request, he stepped aside to allow her entrance. She made her way to a chair and sat down. She drew her shawl more tightly about her.

"I will wake my valet to start a fire," he offered.

"That won't be necessary."

The candle beside his bed remained lit. The light was enough for him to see the shadow of her body through her gown. Her hair fell in curls down her shoulders. He liked the way she looked with her hair down. Walking to the writing desk, he lit another candle to divert his attentions away from her. His body had been primed by their earlier kiss, and he should have masturbated to ease the tension. Now it was too late. He would have to take care of himself after she had left.

"How may I be of service, Countess?" he asked as he leaned against the writing desk, forcing his gaze to her face and away from the soft glow of her bosom. Though the look of her mouth—the supple lips hanging like ripe berries for the picking—did not aid his state.

She seemed disappointed by his question and faltered. She studied her worn slippers. He, too, glanced at her slippers. How he wanted to take her in his arms once more! But instead, he waited with a patience he never knew existed and an uncertainty he had never experienced. He knew his women, could anticipate their actions and reactions—and oftentimes it mattered not what they were for his pursuit would overcome any resistance. With the Countess of Lowry, he was tentative. Perhaps Lady Athena had dealt his confidence a blow earlier, but he knew that to be far too convenient a pretext.

"I have judged you harshly," she said at last. "I should not have."

She came to his room to tell him that? he wondered skeptically. It was no small matter for a woman to knock upon the door of a man in the dead of night.

"They believe us to be husband and wife," she explained as if reading his thoughts.

"And you did not dissuade them from their assumption?" he inquired.

"I had not the opportunity. I had started to with Mrs. Pettigrew, but perhaps it is just as well they presume us to be married. Yes, it is best. It would be otherwise difficult to explain to Mr. Pettigrew…"

Her cheeks grew red referencing their kiss.

"Your secret is safe with me, madam."

"Thank you. I know you not to be without some sense of decency, though my words might lead you to deduce that I think you a worthless wanton when the truth of the matter is—that is, I do not mean to cast aspersions on your character. I do not condone what you do, but you are not immoral for indulging in the—the pleasures of the flesh."

The last words tumbled from her mouth quickly, and she took in a deep breath. He studied her with interest, wondering where her words were intended to lead.

"We are all of us fallible," she continued. "And the, er, pleasures of the flesh is hardly the worst of sins. At least not in my regard. Quite the contrary. I think it a relatively harmless sin compared to greed or a disregard for the fellow man. Or one of the other seven deadly sins, though I cannot think what they are at present."

Phineas curled his fingers around the edge of the writing desk. If she did not reach her conclusion soon, she may not have the opportunity—for a man could only be well-behaved for so long when faced with a half-dressed woman in his room.

"I have not been without sin—that is, I…" She stared once again towards the floor. "I hope you will pardon the disparaging remarks I have made. I am not in the main so critical, but you seem to try my nerves such that I am beside myself. But I—I hope you will pardon me and—and kiss me again."

He nearly slid from the table. She glanced up at him, and he could no sooner deny her than he could the earnest faces of the girls at the asylum even if he did not already have the desire to do just as she wished.

"Are you sure that is what you want, Countess?"

Silence settled between them and he regretted his question and the opportunity he had given her to reconsider her request.

"I wish for you to kiss me," she pronounced more firmly.

Spoken without hesitation, it was almost a command. The blood surged in his groin. He went to stand before her. Taking her hands in his, he lifted her to her feet. He cupped her face, tilted her mouth towards his, and took a deep breath of the nectar he was about to drink. His mouth hovered above hers as he soaked in the anticipation. Then he brushed his lips to hers. Her eyelids flickered and he sensed a sigh from her.

How sweet these lips! Supple as a ripe summer fruit, sweet as the purest Caribbean sugar. He moved his lips deliberately over hers, patiently plumbing the depths of her mouth, his probing tongue leaving no spot unturned. She attempted to return his kiss at first but soon conceded the effort to his mastery. This kiss was his to command. His to lead. She need only succumb.

When he had sufficiently worked her mouth, leaving her wet and breathless, he swept her into his arms and carried her to his bed. There he continued the kiss, less tenderly and more forcefully this time. He trailed his mouth along her jaw, then to the soft area beneath it. Her back arched in response, pushing her bosom against his chest. He kissed and sucked the top of her neck, just below the ear. She let out a lilting gasp. Playfully he nipped her earlobe before digging his mouth down the side of her neck and tonguing the length of her collar bone. He tossed aside her shawl and pulled down the flimsy fabric of her gown to reveal her breast.

Heavenly, he thought to himself as he stared at the large brown areolas, somehow familiar to him. The nipples, already hardened, pointed boldly at him. He licked his bottom lip before encasing a teasing nipple with his mouth. He swirled his tongue against the little nub and elicited a whispered moan from her. Cupping the bottom of the breast, he pushed the orb more fully into his mouth. He took as much of the flesh into his mouth as he could. Soon his suckling had her writhing into the bedsheets. Her pelvis pressed against him, making him all too aware of the tightness in his own groin. But his desire would have to wait.

Her stays laced in the front, and he went back to kissing her upon the mouth as he untied them. He pushed her gown down past her shoulders, which he caressed with his lips. He freed the other breast and took it into his mouth. The candle beside his bed sputtered its last, but not before he noticed the mark beneath the nipple. How curious…

He was tempted to light another candle for a closer look, but he had worked her into a light frenzy. Her panting and moaning had become one. Reaching beneath the hem of her gown, he skimmed his hand along her leg. When he brushed against her thigh, she shivered. He moved his hand across the smoothness of her belly before nestling between her legs. He waited to see if she would object. She stiffened but said nothing. He brushed his thumb against the nub of flesh between her folds. She was more than damp, her desire having pooled quite a reservoir between her thighs. He stroked her clitoris lightly. Her body relaxed, and she murmured her pleasure. Gently he grazed the clitoris with his thumb and fondled it between the knuckles of his forefinger, gradually increasing the pressure as he saw her pleasure mounting.

He began rubbing her more vigorously, though he sensed some of her tension had returned. Her brows knit in concentration, and her body seemed poised above the precipice but did not spend.

"Pray do not persist if you should tire," she mumbled.

He stared at her. Phineas Barclay had never left a woman unsatiated. But he tentatively ceased his ministrations. She whimpered.

"Do not resist the inevitable," he said softly into her ear as he passed his finger across her pleasure bud. "Surrender to the pleasure…for it is pleasurable, is it not?"

She nodded vigorously.

"Ease your mind…let the flesh indulge in what nature has imbued in our bodies…"

Her fingers curled into the sheets beneath her. He could see her attempting to comply, but a part of her still resisted. Her climax was no easy matter. He could not remember one as challenging save for his early years as a lover, before he knew how to read a woman's body. Still strumming his fingers against her, he lapped at her breasts once more. How familiar they felt.

Rising onto his knees, he removed his banyan, then dove his face between her thighs. She yelped in surprise, but he held fast to her thighs with both hands. Taking in her delectable musk, he pressed his tongue between her folds. She quivered. He licked and teased until the wetness of her desire coated him, mouth and jaw. He found the spot that elicited the greatest gasps and extorted it mercilessly. Her body erupted in spasms, her thighs knocked against his ears, and a cry tore from her throat. He wrung the last of her climax from her before easing off his tongue.

His ardor stretched painfully in triumph, but he needed to see that she fared well. When she opened her eyes, they seemed to glisten with tears. She gave him a meek smile.

"Thank you," she said.

What an odd thing to say, he considered.

"I am fortunate you are…persistent," she added.

"Has it been that long since last you spent?" he asked. "Do you not pleasure yourself?"

"I—it requires some time," she answered. Despite the darkness, he knew her to be blushing.

"Show me."

"Wh…"

"Show me how you pleasure yourself."

She hesitated but then reached two fingers between her legs. She stroked herself a few times, then retracted her hand. He caught her hand and returned it to her quim.

"Do not stop."

He heard her swallow, but she obliged, timidly caressing herself. He undid her stays completely and freed her body from its confines. At last he could see the full shape of her. The voluptuous curve of her hips. The subtle swell of her belly. He caressed her through her nightgown. Her stroking became more earnest. Locking his lips to hers, he reached his hand to join her hand. They bumped hands but soon found a fitting division of labor. She attended the top of her clitoris while he strummed the bottom. He slid his finger into her cunnie. Her body arched off the bed as she spent, her other hand grasping his arm. After a few final jerks, her body settled back into the sheets.

Her face glowed with tiny beads of perspiration dotting her forehead and nose. Her cheeks had a beautiful flush. Even the disarray of her hair added to her appeal. He would have her looking thusly always. She took many breaths before smiling once more at him. If any man could see her now, he would not deem Gertie Farrington to be plain. She was lovely, and Phineas felt his heart swell to think that he alone might be privy to this beauty.

She sat up. "And now I believe you to merit some attention."

"That is unnecessary, Countess," he replied, but she had already crawled onto her knees and approached his still stiffened rod. "My glory was to see you spend. I can care for myself."

"But that would not be as pleasurable," she objected, reaching for his erection.

It pulsed at her touch. Before he could utter another word, her mouth had descended upon him. He groaned as warm wetness engulfed his member. She swallowed him as if practiced in the art. Where and how could she have attained such a skill? But his capacity to think ebbed away as she moved her mouth up and down his shaft in a scintillating rhythm. He threaded a hand into her hair, wanting nothing more than to thrust his hips harder at her and drive himself as far down her throat as he could. He would never have guessed to find Lady Lowry on her hands and knees performing fellatio as if she were a common strumpet. With more exuberance than a common strumpet...

With great reluctance, he eased her off of him. Her lips glistened, and a small string of saliva hung between her mouth and the head of his shaft.

"Countess, pray do not be obligated—" he began.

She stared up at him with large, earnest eyes.

"Ravish me," she said.

* * * * *

The words echoed through her own ears as if a foreign voice had uttered them, and Gertie could tell that her directive had caught Barclay by surprise, but she felt no hesitation. His obvious arousal had lifted her confidence, and she knew when first she knocked upon his door what she intended, what she wanted. The wine had worn off, and still the desire had remained. Their kiss had lingered with her for hours, burning her body, a flame that she could not quell despite her best efforts to sort her thoughts into tidy analyses.

It was not her body alone that wanted Barclay.

As upsetting as his words had been, she had to acknowledge the truth of what he said. That he could so clearly state her situation in life pained and embarrassed her, but she sensed his empathy – which he had dubbed 'pity,' and for that she was furious. The great Lady Athena merited no pity! But he knew not Lady Athena. He saw only a meek little wife of the Earl of Lowry. That he should still attend to her, that he should move himself to kiss her, had done much to excite a part of her that even Lady Athena had not experienced.

Why should she not indulge herself? And if she were to commit adultery, why not with the man who excelled in such affairs? Perhaps she had crossed that line when she became Lady Athena. Even were she not a patron of *Madame Botreaux's*, Alexander had not chosen to stay faithful. And though two wrongs did not make a right, why should she play the dutiful, self-sacrificing wife? And why did it take Lord Barclay of all people to make her question herself? Then there was the simple fact that she wanted the sinful and seductive Lord Barclay. She had wanted him the first time she saw him in the Bennington library. Her head ruled the day then, but now these raw, primal feelings burning inside her would not go quietly into the night.

"Fuck me," she said again.

A muscle rippled along his jaw. She reached for him, hoping to urge his assent with a few strokes, but he caught her wrist and pushed her back into the pillows. He covered her body with his and kissed her. Her body exalted at the weight upon her. His hand reached between her legs, though he had no need to arouse her further. She was still wet there, and her cunnie fair ached with the desire to be filled. He brushed his length against her clitoris and coated it with her wetness. She nearly screamed for him to enter her.

She groaned in satisfaction when at last he pushed the head of his rod into her cunnie. He grunted at her tightness. She thrust her hips up at him, encouraging him to continue. Slowly, he slid himself further into her as if worried that he might break her. She gasped at the intrusion filling her and held tightly onto his arms. His erection pulsed, stretching her even more. She closed her eyes, willing herself to relax and reminding herself that the pain would diminish.

"My God," he murmured when at last he had buried himself to the hilt. He planted light kisses upon her eyelids.

She flexed her cunnie about his shaft. He responded by withdrawing completely. She let out a cry of protest. How empty she felt without him nestled inside her…

Opening her eyes, she looked at him. Had something gone wrong? What thought had infiltrated his head to prevent him from—

He shoved his himself back inside of her, grinding his pubis into hers. The angle of his thrusting pulled at the nerves of her engorged clitoris. The initial discomfort had faded and beautiful sensations took its place. His rhythmic thrusting coaxed wave after wave of pleasure. She nearly squealed in delight. She reveled in how fully hefilled her. The yearning ache consumed her entire body, making her want to meld into him as one.

When her gasps became more agitated, he quickened the motion of his hips. The bed shuddered against the wall with the force of his efforts. A beautiful sweat encased his body. But she had little time to admire his form. That pleasurable ache, emanating from deep inside her belly, shattered into tremors of pure delight that tore through her from head to toe. She bucked against him uncontrollably as her climax pushed through her body.

She heard what sounded like a growl from him, felt his length shoving harder and deeper into her, then felt the liquid warmth of his seed filling her. His legs jerked against her in his release, and he allowed himself to collapse onto her, his chest flattening her breasts below. She wound an arm around his neck and held him close. And she would have been content to remain as she was if time could stand still.

CHAPTER TWELVE

THEY MADE LOVE once more before the sunrise. Gertie had stirred against him in the middle of the night. His ardor had responded instantly despite his being in a state of half-sleep. Pulling the nightgown down over her hips, he tended to her quim once more with his tongue, cultivating her most sensitive spot on the left side of her engorged bud, until she begged for him. He thrust into her with a renewed appetite, as if they had not had congress but two hours before, as if his member tasted of her wet warmth for the first time. How tight she still was, how exquisite the pressure of her cunnie about his shaft…

The rain clouds muted the brightness of day, leaving the room dim and grey. Phineas listened to the steady patter of rain against the window as Gertie slept in the crook of his arm. He could feel her breath upon his chest. Once more his erection reared its head. But he was content to lie as they were and would not disturb her from her peaceful slumber. He prayed it would rain for days.

Gertie purred and her eyelids fluttered. She nestled herself closer to him, then woke with a start as if she had forgotten where she was. She turned to look at him.

"Good morning," he smiled.

She relaxed into a smile, but he could see her mind beginning to churn. "I should—I should return to my room before the servants discover me."

"I thought they believed us to be husband and wife?" he inquired, running a hand through her thick tresses and massaging the back of her head.

"I think that to be the polite assumption. I doubt they believe it as you arrived with your valet upon horseback, and I arrived sans servants in a post-chaise."

"What does it matter what they believe?"

"It...nonetheless, I think I had best retire to my own room."

She had managed to wrap a sheet about herself, but he had no intention of letting her go before he verified an important matter. Last night he had thought he had seen a discoloration to the left of her nipple, but the lighting had been poor, and he had been too engrossed to study it more closely.

"Do you regret what has happened?"

She hesitated. "I—no. I came of my own volition. But I—it is rather early to form regrets. Do—do you?"

In response, he brought her head to his until their lips met. He rolled on top of her, pinning her body below his, as he continued to kiss her, leaving no doubts as to how he felt. She gasped upon feeling his hardened length against her thigh.

"I want more of you, Countess," he said into her neck as he caressed a shoulder and left kisses about her collar.

He tore the bed sheet away from her bosom and stared at the birthmark upon her breast. The blood pounded in his head.

Lady Athena.

He wondered how the fact could have escaped him all this time. His gaze went to her mouth. Of course. How had he failed to recognize those amazing lips? He had always suspected there was more to Gertie than met the eye, but he had never imagined uncovering a secret as grand as this. And then he wanted her more fully, more deeply than he had ever wanted to possess another being. His gaze met hers, and the obvious lust reflected in her eyes made his ardor stretch to its limits.

His mouth descended upon the informing breast. The vigor with which he claimed her made her gasp. He grasped the nipple between his teeth, then sucked it hard until her back arched off the bed. Cupping both breasts in his hands, he kneaded the glorious orbs. She would not find it easy to leave his bed.

"The servants—" she said in a meek attempt to halt their passions.

"My valet knows better than to allow anyone to disturb me whilst I am occupied."

Her eyes widened. "He knows?"

"Francis is very discreet," he assured her, "and has been in my service during the whole of my time on the Continent."

He returned to mauling her breasts with his mouth. He slid a hand between her thighs, sticky from their efforts during the night but coated with fresh wetness. Soon he had her writhing and panting. This time he plunged into her with little ceremony. Making love to Lady Lowry was entirely different from conquering the Lady Athena. He considered all the torment of waiting and wanting he had endured at the hands of Lady Athena, and he shoved his ardor into Gertie with more force than he had intended.

It was still Gertie he was with, he reminded himself. He eased off of her and gently kissed her about the face.

"No woman has wished to leave my bed before," he informed her.

She smiled devilishly. "Are you so confident in your skills, sir?"

He returned her smile, then flipped her onto her stomach. He pulled her arse up for a better angle. Her pink folds glistened with her lust. He wondered if one day he might penetrate her arse—an ultimate victory with Lady Athena. For now, he pushed himself at her quim. She grunted in satisfaction as he slid inside her. Wrapping an arm around the front of her thigh, he plied her clitoris until she let out moan after moan of pleasure. He varied the tempo of his thrusting, easing off the first time she began to ascend towards her climax—a small nod to Hephaestus.

But he could not deny Gertie for long. He reveled too much in her spending. Pulling back, he shoved himself at her buttocks and felt his cods swing up against her flesh. Her face—one half buried in her pillow, the other half covered by her hair—could not be viewed, but he needed only to hear her groans to know that she was close to her release. She clawed at the sheets below her. Then the paroxysm of ecstasy overcame her. She let out a helpless wail.

He could have spent, but he held back the release boiling in his groin. He wanted to pound her senseless. Such that she would never conceive of leaving his bed. Flipping her onto her back, he threw her legs over his shoulders and plunged into the depths of her womb. The heat of her cunnie seared his shaft. There was much he could do to her, and he wanted to do it all. But he had no wish to frighten her. He needed her to feel safe and secure. Grasping her wrists, he pulled her arms overhead.

"My God, Gertie," he breathed, "you are wondrous."

"You've no need to feign civilities with me," she responded as she ground herself to the best of her ability.

There were women who possessed more skill at lovemaking than she. He could tell that she was not practiced in the positions of fornication. But it mattered not. She felt marvelous to him.

"I have never lied to a woman, Gertie."

"Never?"

"I've not had a need to."

"Y-yes. I understand why."

As her second climax waved over, her eyes rolled towards the back of her head. She jerked against him. Her cunnie pulsed madly about him. The pressure in his abdomen was too much. Grabbing her legs, he shoved himself at her and pumped his seed inside of her. He shuddered as the effects of his climax shot down both of his legs. How was it possible that this time seemed even more glorious than the ones before? He lay beside her and pulled her to him.

"I wonder that I shall be able to walk after this?" she wondered aloud.

He smiled. "That was but a small sampling of the possibilities."

* * * * *

Gertie's head swam with the excitement of what she had done. What frightened her a little was that she yearned for *more*.

Her stomach grumbled.

"I think breakfast would be in order?" Barclay suggested.

Too embarrassed to look him in the eye, she nodded. He cupped her chin and forced her gaze to his.

"No regrets."

"No regrets," she echoed.

"Francis can have a plate brought to your room if you wish."

He gathered her articles and wrapped his banyan about her. Then he opened the door and glanced out into the hallway. He motioned for her. Clutching her garments tightly to her, she scurried through the opening.

"Gertie."

She turned and was met with the fullness of his mouth upon

hers. He seared a kiss upon her, one that tingled her lips long after, before letting her go. She ran into the sanctuary of her own room, her spirits soaring. How she loved the sound of her name upon his lips! How she loved his lips—and all the delightful things he did to her with them! She pulled his banyan tighter about her and felt as if he held her still. She could hardly wait to see him again.

"What a giddy girl you've become!" she admonished her reflection in the mirror, but she was too happy to care.

She hummed to herself as she went through her trunk, trying to find the best outfit, one that might catch his eye. She sighed remembering how his eyes sparkled, how beautiful and mesmerizing they were. No wonder he could cast his spells upon so many women.

"Breakfast, my lady," Mrs. Pettigrew announced with a knock at the door.

Gertie devoured the offering of eggs, ham, and bread with relish.

"How radiant my lady looks this morning," Mrs. Pettigrew commented. "And yesterday you looked as wretched as a drowned mouse. I trust you had a pleasant night?"

Gertie nodded with her eyes downward cast.

"He's a right handsome man that husband of yours. And charming as sin."

She dared to study the innkeeper's wife but could discern nothing from the woman's face. Barclay's words echoed in her ears. Why should it matter what these strangers thought? Should she care if they should cast disapproving glances her way? Yet she did not relish having to live a lie whilst she resided in the inn.

"He's not my husband," she braved.

"A pity," Mrs. Pettigrew replied nonchalantly as she reviewed Gertie's garments. "Wouldn't mind waking to his countenance each morning."

Gertie smiled and allowed Mrs. Pettigrew to brush out her hair.

"I wonder that he will ever marry," Gertie said. "He has no fondness for the institution of matrimony."

"I thought him a bit of a rogue."

He might be all rogue, Gertie considered to herself.

"But a rogue can be tamed—by the right mistress."

Gertie thought about Lady Athena. Could she tame one of the most infamous rakes and debauchers? She fingered her wedding band. Even if she could, there was little to be done whilst she was married to Alexander.

After completing her toilette, she went downstairs and found Barclay in the drawing room. Dressed in a fitting pair of buff breeches, his fine linen, a striped waistcoat, and a lace-trimmed cravat, he was a feast for the eyes. *And* he looked every bit as seductive without his refined garments, she thought to herself, recalling his naked body, the perfect subject for any painter or sculptor. If she had not been so taken by his kisses, she would have taken the time to caress every ridge of his chest and torso, the curve of muscle in his legs, and the tightness of his arse.

"Countess," he greeted with a bow. "Care to join me in a game of *vingt-et-un*?"

"I suppose that would be harmless enough."

He pulled out a chair for her. "If I may, you look lovely."

She blushed like a young thing who had just had her come-out. "I saw the way you examined my gown. It does not meet with your approval."

"I would it were as appealing as that which it adorns."

She hesitated, not knowing how to respond for she was not rehearsed in receiving compliments. She scooped up the cards at the table and began to shuffle them. "I suppose when next I venture to Mayfair, I ought request your company that you may advise me on what to buy."

He inclined his head. "I should be happy to be of service, madam."

They played their first two hands without exchanging words. It was charitable of him to be so cordial to her, but then, it only made sense as they were trapped in the inn together for an indefinite amount of time. She wondered if his behavior would differ if he knew he did not have to face her again the following morning?

She glanced at him to find him studying her. She shifted uncomfortably. Those eyes of his were both enthralling and unsettling.

"Shall we enhance the game with a wager?" he inquired.

"I have not much in the way of funds upon me," she replied as she dealt the cards.

"A wager of a different nature."

She was about to peer at her cards when he put a hand over hers.

"Have you ever been bound?"

Her mouth went dry. "Bound?"

"Tied."

Her gulp was audible. "No."

"Bondage can often enhance the pleasure."

She said nothing. Her heart throbbed against her ribs, feeling as if he had discerned her secret somehow.

"Is this part of your customary seduction?" she stalled.

"Not at all," he said, his gaze pinning her in her seat. "But you strike me as someone who would dare to experiment with the adventurous."

"Indeed?"

That surprised her. She had never thought anyone would consider her daring. "And w-why do you think that, Lord Barclay?"

"People are not always what they seem, Lady Lowry."

She sucked in her breath. "What is the wager you propose?"

"If I win this hand, I will have the privilege of rigging you."

"And if I win?"

He grinned. "You may bind me."

Something stirred in her loins. She looked him in the eyes. "Very well."

He removed his hand, and she looked at her cards. A queen and a six. Not the best hand, but she had the advantage of going second. She waited for him, but he shook his head. Damn. That meant he had a decent hand. She would have to take the chance. She gave herself another card. A seven. Damnation. He revealed his hand—a ten and five.

"I promise you will not regret having lost," he assured her.

Her pulse quickened.

"You have done such things?" she inquired carefully.

"Yes."

"What have you done?"

"With light bondage, I would bind the wrists together, overhead or behind the back. For the more experienced partner, I might tie the heels to the thighs, lay you across a table, and fuck you from behind."

She squirmed in her seat. "I think that I shall retire upstairs for a brief respite."

He grinned. "How coincidental. I, too, have a mind to retire upstairs."

* * * * *

He followed her up the stairs to her room. When he had closed the door behind him, she turned towards him. He smothered her with a deep and probing kiss. Her desire permeated the air and in the ardor with which she returned his kiss.

"Remove your clothing," he ordered.

"But I have not been long in them," she protested.

"I will have you naked, my Countess."

She hesitated.

"Come, I will assist you."

Together they removed the pins and untied the various parts of her gown. He caressed the parts of her skin laid bare. After unlacing her stays, he stepped back and watched as she did the rest. The throbbing in his shaft intensified when she slid the stockings from her legs. She stood naked but for her chemise. She looked at him.

"Surely you are not overcome with modesty?" he asked as he did an appreciative sweep of her body. "I do not think you had forgotten last night."

She blushed.

"Would you rather I ripped the chemise from your body?"

There was a hitch in her breath. Dutifully, she let fall the chemise. It pooled about her ankles. Circling around her, he could sense her desire to cover herself. Perhaps it were easier for her in the dimness of night than to expose herself in the glare of day. No matter. She would overcome her timidity with him.

He began to unloosen his cravat while she stood naked and uncomfortable. After he had slid off his waistcoat and discarded his breeches, he reached for her and molded her bare body to him.

"What—what else might you do when binding a lover?" she asked.

"I could wind the ropes about your breasts…" He traced where the ropes would have been with his finger. "…and secure them tightly so that they protruded for me to feed upon."

Her bosom swelled. The thought aroused her, eh? As he suspected, Lady Athena was no impartial observer or commander, as she sometimes acted.

"And?"

"What would you have me do, Countess?"

She thought for a moment and he wondered if he had pushed too far.

"Tie my limbs to the corners of the bed?" she suggested.

"And should I bind your mouth to prevent you from speaking or crying for help?"

She nodded. He cupped a hand about one butt cheek.

"And should I use your body to mine content? And punish you an' you did not do as I command?"

He slapped her derriere. She yelped in surprise, then reached for his length. It, too, was beginning to respond to their musings.

"Before I reward you with what you desire," he began, leading her to the bed, "you will take me into your mouth. Lie upon your back that I may have full access to your breasts."

She did as he instructed. With her head hanging slightly off the edge of the bed, she guided him into her mouth. The member was still partially soft but became rigid quickly inside her mouth. She lapped at it greedily.

"Pleasure yourself," he directed, "but do not spend without my word."

He could hardly believe that he stood with the Countess of Lowry taking in his erection while she fondled herself. It was but yesterday that he thought Gertie would despise him for all eternity. He caressed her breasts, running his thumbs over her nipples, pinching them. She let out a muffled cry into his groin and gagged upon him. He gently slapped a breast. She resumed her fellatio. He tapped at the inside of her thigh. She jumped, but her fingers commenced a more furious caress upon herself.

The vision of her body sprawled upon the bed, her luscious lips locked about himwas enough to make him want to spend in an instant. He pulled himself out of her mouth before he sprayed his seed down her throat.

"On your hands and knees," he directed as he walked to the other side of the bed.

She obeyed without hesitation, presenting him with her arse. He caressed the soft surface of her derriere, then gave it a sharp slap. The flesh quivered. He smacked the cheek again and watched as it began to blush. He reached between her thighs to fondle her clitoris.

"There are places in London where men and women can indulge their most secret desires," he said.

She only moaned to his ministrations.

"Do you know of such places?"

When she did not answer, he pinched a labia. She yelped.

"Yes—I have heard of such places."

He resumed his caresses. She ground herself into his hand.

"Have you had a desire to visit one of them?"

She could have simply lied, but she chose to stall. He slapped her arse to prompt her.

"Y-Yes."

"What would you do there?"

"Beg you to take me."

He felt a surge of warmth. His arousal could no longer resist. He shoved himself into her. She cried out in satisfaction. Grabbing her hips, he plumbed the depths of her womb with his shaft. Her arse flesh trembled every time it slapped against his pelvis.

"Yes! Yes!" she cried as she slammed into him.

She spent quickly, her arms buckling beneath her. He continued to pummel her until his own climax rushed through him. His rod throbbed as the warm liquid of his desire poured forth into her. How marvelous she felt. How marvelous he felt inside of her. Gently, he disengaged himself and lay down beside where she had collapsed. He reached for her and she nestled herself into his arms.

"These places that you speak of," she murmured, the glow of her climax still upon her face, "do you frequent them, Lord Barclay?"

"On occasion."

He considered revealing that he had been to *Madame Botreaux's*, but he knew not if it would upset her. He was sure that she found safety in her anonymity. Better to wait to see if she spoke of it first.

"Do you take your lovers there?"

"If they are partial to such…activities." He kissed the tips of her fingers. "I would take you there, Countess."

She took a sharp breath and changed the subject. "They must think us a pair of rabbits at this inn."

"Do you always consider what others are thinking?"

"Do you never consider what others are thinking?" she retorted.

"Seldom."

She shook her head, then turned to look at him. He cradled one side of her head in his hand and allowed her to study him. He brushed a thumb across her cheeks. He knew of no one who wore a natural blush as well as she.

"I cannot fathom why I do not completely detest you," she remarked.

"Only half detest."

"Yes, well, you are an unabashed debaucher and a…"

"I believe the word you ascribed to me is 'murderer.'"

"I take it you did not mean to kill Jonathan Weston? That must be why his seconds bear you no ill will? They understood it to be an accident."

His jaw tightened. He had not had to fully recall that event in recent years. He looked into her earnest patient eyes. She wanted to know. And for the first time, he wanted someone else to know.

"I had no intention of killing Jonathan," he admitted. "I agreed to the duel knowing that I could draw first blood. I had but to prick his arm and it would all be over within minutes and no one the wiser. It had rained the night before, much like the rains now. The grounds at Putney Common were like mush beneath our feet.

"As expected, I drew blood. I grazed his shoulder with my sword. The seconds proclaimed an end to the duel. I turned away from Jonathan to hand my sword to my friend Lord Bertram. I heard one of the other seconds call my name in alarm. Turning, I saw Jonathan come at me with sword still in hand. I saw the rage in his eyes, and I knew he meant to kill me. I fended off his initial attack. Our seconds attempted to reason with him, but I knew he would not rest until I lay dead. Though the better swordsman was I, Jonathan had a crazed ardor. My heel slipped on a sodden patch, and I went down. Jonathan charged. I parried and thrust my sword at him. It went through his heart."

Gertie had covered her mouth. He wondered if he had worsened matters by telling her. He waited tensely for her to speak.

"Why have you not spoken of this?" she asked. "Why did your seconds not explain? Had it been known that you were only defending yourself, surely you would not have had to live in exile?"

The wrenching emotions from five years ago threatened to wash over him as if it had been but yesterday.

"I killed a man, Gertie."

"Yes, but he should not have tried to kill you—and with your back turned!"

She grabbed his hand between her own, and that alone gave him the strength to resist the pain of the past. He took a breath of relief. She did not condemn him. But there was one last truth to be told...

"Everyone should know what occurred!" she insisted.

"It would not change the outcome."

"But—but I was convinced you were in the wrong. I thought you a horrible monster."

Her eyes glistened with tears of remorse.

"You were not wrong to think it," he comforted.

"All this time I had pitied Jonathan Weston! I can understand his anger over being made a cuckold, I can understand his wanting satisfaction, but to try to kill you..."

A new pressure built in his chest. He would risk losing the tenderness he had just earned—a painful prospect—but a part of him wanted her of all people to know the complete truth.

"Jonathan wished to kill me because he was in pain," he explained. "Not because of my affair with his wife, to which he was a party."

A quixotic expression came over her.

"He often watched us. At times, I would invite him to take his wife while I watched. But in the course of the affair, I became aware that Jonathon had more of an interest in me than his wife. I believe he had fallen in love with me."

She lowered her gaze pensively. He tried not to startle her with any movement, though it tore at him not to know how she felt.

"Thus, you must not judge Jonathan too harshly," he added.

Strange, but it felt like tears pressing against his eyes. He could not remember when he had last cried. She looked up at the instant when he struggled the most against the tide of his emotions.

"You have a rare charity, Phineas," she said softly.

This time he could not help himself. He wrapped his arms about her, pulling her tightly to him, feeling as if holding her could right the world. He blinked away the tears and felt the pressure unravel from his chest.

"Do you still think me a monster?"

"You are monstrous at times but no monster. Indeed, I am now convinced your bosom harbors redeeming qualities—at least one worth counting."

"Impudent minx."

He tilted her chin up towards him and kissed her. They made love sweetly and tenderly to the sound of rain pattering against the window. It was not enough for him to caress her and bring her pleasure. It was not enough to feel himself deep inside her. The wealth of emotion that consumed him needed an outlet through her. It seemed as if he would have to make love to her the rest of his life to feel satiated.

And for a moment he longed for nothing more than just such an opportunity.

Chapter Thirteen

"The rains have stopped," Gertie noted the following morning with a sense of disappointment. She nestled her naked body closer to Phineas as they lay in bed.

"It will still take some time for the roads to dry," he said as he wrapped an arm about her shoulder.

"Ah, then you may not rid yourself of my company so easily," she teased.

"My dear, I have not the slightest wish to do as you claim."

"Surely you have another conquest lying in wait—this 'friend' you are visiting?"

He paused. "She can wait."

The displeasure in his voice made her wonder if she had asked an invasive question, but then he had seemed a man who comfortable speaking about anything. She found herself wondering who this lady friend of his was.

"And now, Lady Lowry," he said, "there is the matter of the wager that you lost."

Her eyes widened. "I thought we had settled the matter of our wager?"

"Did I actually bind you?"

She thought through what had transpired the day before. She had lost at vingt-et-un, she had performed fellatio upon him, they had had dinner together and enjoyed a relaxing afternoon reading by the fire. After a light supper, they had retired to his room, he had pinned her against the wall and fucked her there. She shivered at the memory.

"I suppose not," she answered.

He got out of bed and went to retrieve his cravat, the sash

from his banyan, and two of her stockings. She felt her skin tingle in anticipation. Returning to the bed, he took one of her ankles, wrapped the stocking about it, and tied it to a corner bedpost. He did the same to her other ankle. The rigging forced her legs apart, exposing her quim. He admired the view for a moment before moving to her wrists, binding each to a post until she was stretched to all fours corners of the bed.

"Lovely," he murmured as he stood back to observe his work.

She noticed his erection was as stiff as one of the bedposts she was bound to. She admired his body—the ridges of his chest and abdomen, the tight curve of his arse, the swell of the muscles in his upper arms and legs. She was reminded of Hephaestus, whose body had also made her salivate. She had not thought much of the male form until her patronage at *Madame Botreaux's*. With Phineas Barclay, she longed to caress all parts of him. How beautiful he would have looked bound in Lady Athena's favorite alcove…A strange sense of familiarity overcame her. Had she dreamed just such a thing, for the vision flashing before her felt so vivid.

A slap on her inner thigh snapped her attention back to Phineas.

He ran a knuckle along the arch of her foot. "Your body is at my complete mercy, Countess, to use as I will."

Her cunnie throbbed. She tested her bonds. Well tied. It was quite obvious he was no novice at this. But the experience of being tied instead of the one in command was new for her. A part of her found the deprivation of freedom thrilling. Another part became wary of it. She knew not what he would do.

Obtaining another linen, he wound part of it around one hand, took the end with his other hand, then backhanded it against her quim. The linen slapped sharply against her. She gasped and strained against her bonds. He slapped her quim again. The attention to her most private part made her feel incredibly vulnerable. She wondered if she should be enjoying it. Would Lady Athena be aghast if she did?

"Perhaps if you are good," he said, "I will allow you to rig *me* to the bed."

The thought perked her.

Phineas stroked her clitoris and soon had her panting and

writing. He dipped two fingers into her sodden cunnie. She flexed against him to indicate her desire. He pulled out of her and walking to the head of the bed, he pushed his digits into her mouth.

"Suck," he instructed.

The musky, slightly salty flavor did not agree with her, but she did as he bade, licking his fingers clean of her juices.

He straddled her across the ribs. She saw the head of his rod glistening with the first drops of his semen. Reaching back, he covered his fingers once more with her wetness and rubbed it onto himself. He pushed her breasts together and slid his shaft between them.

"There are so many ways to derive pleasure from a woman's body," he commented.

She wanted to tell him to take his pleasure in all the ways, but she was half mesmerized by his thrusting. The head of his erection would peer in and out from between her two orbs. She wondered how it felt for him. How did the flesh of her breasts compare to her cunnie? He pinched and twisted her nipples as he continued to mash her breasts about his length. Her cunnie ached with want of attention.

By the furrow in his brow, she could see that he was close to spending. He felt as hard as her crop's handle, and the rubbing action was beginning to burn as the lubrication wore off. He ceased and positioned his rod at her mouth. She took him in eagerly, suckling him hard and furious in the hopes of being rewarded.

"My word but someone has a voracious appetite," he observed as he popped himself from her mouth.

"Take me," she responded.

"Did you not wish to beg for it?"

"Please, I wish for you to ravish me. Take me, sir, take me."

"I should like to take you anywhere and at any time I wish."

She whimpered. If she were not bound, she would have frigged herself, regardless of what he would do.

Phineas went to kneel between her legs. He pointed the length of his desire at her cunnie. She strained to reach him. He teased her by pushing only the head of his length into her. It was maddening to have so little of him inside of her when her cunnie burned for him. She pulled at her bonds and wriggled to encase more of his shaft, but the breadth of her movement were confined by the bondage and he was situated too far.

She groaned in frustration. "Please, I must have you. *Please.*"

He plunged inside of her. She squealed in delight. He pumped himself vigorously into her as he lashed the strip of linen against her breasts or backhanded them with his bare hands. The smarting of her breasts, contrasted with the waves of pleasure pulsing from her groin, was exhilarating. She did not know which sensation to focus her mind until the two seemed to fuse as one, sending her body over the precipice of control. Her body jerked against her restraints as if stabbed by ecstasy. She felt a warm stream of liquid filling her, his hot seed spilling inside of her.

When their bodies had ceased to shake against each other, he reached over and unloosened her bonds.

"Care to lose another hand at cards?" he inquired.

She smiled wanly at him. She would lose a hundred hands to this man. There was nothing more she wanted at the moment than Phineas Barclay, body and soul.

She would ignore the sobering thought that it was not to be.

* * * * *

It was with some heaviness of heart that Phineas bore the news that the roads had dried enough to be traveled upon. His only consolation was that Gertie, too, seemed less than pleased. They sat alone in the dining room after their breakfast as her driver prepared the chaise.

"You will not—you will not speak of what happened here to anyone?" she ventured.

"'Pon my honor, wild horses could not drag your name from me."

She pressed her lips together.

"You doubt my word," he deduced.

"It is only...you have had so many liaisons...and everyone knows of your conquests..."

"There are many more that are unknown."

He tilted her chin towards him. "Alas, my dear, you cannot take back what has happened. You may trust me or not. I can only offer you my word."

She nodded. "I understand."

"Do you wish you could undo what has happened?"

"No, but I suppose I had not fully considered the consequences. Even were you to keep your word, the servants might talk."

"Francis would not have survived in my employ if I could not trust him completely. As for those at this inn, you could not have chosen a more discreet location for your assignation."

"I had no intention of seducing you, sir!" she protested. "Would you believe that I deliberately orchestrated losing the wheel to my chaise?"

He laughed. "Have you never attempted to seduce another man? Or harbored thoughts of doing so?"

"I have been devoted to my husband till now," she said simply.

"Have you, Countess?"

She squirmed and glanced away. "I have not been unfaithful," she restated.

"And how do you define faithfulness?"

He thought of all that she must have done at *Madame Boreatux's*. Alexander would have locked her up in Bedlam if he ever found out, but even a more reasoned husband would not have approved.

"I have not been free of lust," she relented.

"Is that all?"

"And I have not taken any man to bed."

"And thus you may claim to be a faithful wife—because you have not copulated?"

"Yes—but you have ruined me now."

He grinned. "Why have you been the faithful wife? If you have lusted for one that was not your husband, why did you not attempt to seduce him? Why remain devoted to Alexander?"

He sensed a little of the ire that she had exhibited the first night he had talked of her husband. They both knew what he had left unsaid this time: that Alexander was not worthy of such loyalty.

"It is different for men," she defended.

"And is that fair?"

"Of course not."

"Then why succumb to unfair standards?"

"I have not. I have lifted my skirts to you of all people!"

"Should I be flattered or offended?"

His words appeared to relax her.

"The ruling on that remains unknown," she taunted.

He looked at her with frank intensity. "Why did you marry Alexander?"

"Because he was a good prospect."

"And?"

"If you must know, I was not one who could attract many such prospects as he. His attentions flattered me and my vanity."

"Were you in love with him?"

"No, I think I knew even then that I was not. But I believed my affections for him would grow. He need not have been the perfect husband. So many men are barely considered decent husbands. I thought—I thought if I had a child, it would not matter if he were a miserable husband. I should have someone I could love—and who would love me. That is the marvelous thing about children: they are so willing to give of their love. Perhaps that is why I want the appearance of a good wife. I will not have any slander upon me visited upon my child."

"Is that why you are a patron of the orphan asylum? Because those girls have become like your children?"

"Yes."

"And why did you alter your course with me?"

"I have not. I am determined to have a child and as bright and happy a future as can be had for him—or her. I think I should be delighted if it should be a girl."

He smiled. "You should have a daughter. A little one as beautiful and steadfast as her mother."

She seemed to catch her breath, and the shine in her eyes made him swell with tenderness. He reached across the table and curled his hand about hers.

"And what would you name this daughter of yours?"

The thought of a name delighted her. "It would be no ordinary name, but something rare and special."

"The name of a goddess perhaps? One whose qualities you admire? Artemis or Athena…"

She frowned. "No, nothing so fanciful, though I like the

goddess Athena most among all the Greek gods."

"For her wisdom or her imperviousness to the powers of Aphrodite?"

"Both. But I would not wish for my daughter to be untouched by love if it could bring her happiness."

"And if it could not? Love is the greatest venture of chance. The odds are never known."

"'So dear I love him that with him, all deaths I could endure. Without him, live no life,'" she quoted. "I wonder that love can so alter the value of life, such is its power?"

"Do you envy Juliet her Romeo?"

"I know not. I have yet to be in love. I have resigned myself that love, of the amorous kind, shall not come. Indeed, it would be useless as I am married."

"Marriage need not prevent love."

"You speak as if you are an advocate of love, but surely you scoff at such sentiment?"

"I have been in love," he replied. "And I have lost. My first love was when I was six and ten—to a woman older and wiser—and married. She had only a fleeting tenderness for me and soon cast me aside for a new lover. I thought I would die from my broken heart. My second love was when I was twenty. She was a lovely young maid, and I meant to court her with the intention of marrying her, but her family wanted nothing of me or my family. Since then, as with you, I find little use for love."

"You have adopted the practices of your mother and father."

"Yes, my older sister Abigail and I have not fallen far from the tree, as it were. But it may surprise you to know that my mother and father loved one another. I know not when or how their marriage went to ruin, and I suspected they engaged in their liaisons as much out of spite as sport. But when my mother died of the consumption, I would find my father sobbing in his study, clutching a small portrait of her."

"Oh," Gertie sighed sadly. "I think if people knew your family—truly knew them—they would not be so quick to cast aspersions. And you. I was wrong to have judged you so harshly. You are much more than you seem."

He ran his knuckles along her cheek as he looked into her face.

"As are you, Countess."

He was about to rise from his chair to kiss her, but the driver entered then to inform Gertie that her chaise was ready. It startled Phineas to think that he might not secure one last kiss from her. He assisted her with her pelisse, wondering how soon he might see her again.

She turned to look at him, her face a mixture of expressions. For once, he could not discern what a woman was thinking.

"I—I enjoyed your company, Lord Barclay," she said stiffly.

Was that all? Or did she hesitate to say more in the presence of her driver?

He brought her hand to his lips and detected a slight tremor in her. "Shall I escort you to your chaise, madam?"

She nodded. Outside, he cursed the brilliance of the sun that had terminated their tryst. He handed her into the carriage, desperately wanting her to say something to indicate that their days at the Four Horse Posting Inn might not be an isolated affair. Already he could feel a sense of longing pooling in his bosom.

"No regrets," he reminded her as he observed the driver mounting his perch.

"None," she responded.

"*Au revoir*, Countess."

The driver cracked his whip, and the chaise lurched forward.

She had attested to no regrets, but as he watched the chaise departing from view, he had the foreboding that the regrets would come with time, and a time too soon.

CHAPTER FOURTEEN

THE MARCHIONESS OF Dunnesford threw her arms about Gertie. Gertie returned the embrace of the petite, slender woman.

"Motherhood becomes you well!" Gertie sighed when she had pulled away from Harrietta. "You look more striking than when I saw you last!"

The Marchioness was no beauty of the first order, but she had a vitality that shone from her eyes and a warm manner that had put Gertie instantly at ease when first they had met. It was as if Harrietta had sensed Gertie's tension upon being introduced into gentle society as the wife of an Earl, perhaps because she, too, had not been born into the elite. The Marquess had shocked his peers in selecting her for his wife, though he had done it initially from obligation, but his devotion to her now was steadfast. Gertie stood in awe of Harrietta for she found the Marquess a rather intimidating man.

"Let us see the little one," Gertie prompted.

Harrietta led Gertie to the nursery where the baby lay sleeping. He had chestnut hair like his mother.

"Hettie, he is beautiful," Gertie whispered.

"I am blessed, Gertie, for he has the disposition of an angel," Harrietta said.

They tiptoed from the room and went down into a drawing room for tea.

"Now tell me you did not come through that horrible storm?" Harrietta asked after they had been served. "And all without servants? Do you lack funds? I could have a word with Vale. I am sure he could assist--"

"No, pray do not. I manage quite well. We stayed at a rather delightful inn waiting for the rain to pass and the roads to dry."

The Marchioness pounced quickly. "'We?'"

Gertie blushed. "A friend—or not precisely a friend—the wheel came undone from the post-chaise, you see—he happened by—the rain was pouring—"

Harrietta had a bemused look upon her face. Gertie took a deep breath. Of course she could not hide anything from her dearest friend.

"Hettie, I have sinned."

"How delightful! And I thought my dear friend incapable of such a thing."

"Yes, he considers it a tragedy as well," Gertie mumbled as she stared into her tea.

Harrietta shifted to the edge of the rococo settee, one of many exquisite pieces of furniture that graced the drawing room. Gertie suppressed a stab of envy. Harrietta had it all: a beautiful home, a remarkable husband, and now a darling baby boy.

"Something happened at this delightful inn?" Harrietta guessed.

"Yes, but—but it was in passing. It was meaningless."

"But you are blushing, Gertie! I protest I have never seen such gladness in your eyes."

In truth, the memory of it all continued to thrill her, but harboring such feelings was hardly helpful. Perhaps she would indulge only a little in her retelling. She told Harrietta how Barclay had come across her on the road, how they were sequestered in the inn by the rain, and how much he vexed her.

"I could not tolerate him at first," Gertie explained. "I was convinced he had no redeeming qualities, but then…"

She recounted how he had insisted on chaperoning her to the orphan asylum, how he had danced with the little girls, and how he had insisted on accompanying her on future trips into St. Giles.

"He has a kindred heart. I wonder that he might get along with my Vale?" Harrietta commented.

Gertie made no reply. Somehow she did not envision Barclay and the Marquess becoming fast friends.

"I thought perhaps he meant to befriend me that I might agree to a business proposition he had," Gertie said instead. "But then he makes remarks that infuriate me to my wit's end that he cannot possibly have that motivation—or he is an idiot, but I think not for he has had far too many conquests where the fair sex is concerned."

"My dear Gertie has fallen for a rake? This is far too intriguing a man."

"Intriguing that he is a debaucher?"

"Intriguing that he should yet command your admiration and tendre."

"Admiration? I hardly think that I admire him."

"But, Gertie, I know you would not risk your marriage for any mere mortal."

"But I think I am as silly as most of the women who have succumbed to his charms. He has a—a physical prowess that is hard to deny when he presses his advantage. He seduces for sport, and I am but the latest of his diversions. I first met him when he was with—with *Sarah*."

Harrietta wrinkled her nose. "Granted, Sarah is quite the pretty thing, but I would hardly consider her a desirable conquest."

"Perhaps it was my jealousy of her that prompted me to seek his company. Or my distress over learning of Alexander's mistress."

"Then the rumors I heard are true?"

Gertie nodded. Harrietta cursed.

"I feel like a fool," Gertie said. "And I was quite beside myself when I first discovered the matter. Since then, oddly, it has not been as devastating as I expected. What I mourn is the prospect that I shall not have a child, and I do believe that I could be happy with a child to love. Perhaps it is because of these other distractions that I have not had time to lament the state of my marriage."

Harrietta listened raptly to Gertie describing the encounters between Lady Athena and Hephaestus.

"My word, Gertie, you are attracting quite the cadre of men these days!" Harrietta exclaimed after Gertie told her that she had dismissed Hephaestus and did not expect to see him again. "But let us return to this love of yours. Surely you will not dismiss him so easily?"

"Love of mine?" choked Gertie.

"La, dear Gertie, is it not apparent?"

Her cheeks flamed. "I do not think that I love him."

"Love whom?" came a deep tenor from the doorway.

Gertie nearly spilled her tea. At the threshold stood the imposing form of the Marquess of Dunnesford. His dress was nearly as fine as Barclay's, but Vale Aubrey preferred fewer accoutrements. Aubrey did not have the easy, affable smile of Barclay, but his countenance was no less handsome. As with Barclay, he kept himself in formidable shape and possessed the same wide brow and piercing gaze.

The Marquess walked into the room. "Gertie, you are welcome sight. We are pleased that you could stay with us. I hope you ladies will not mind if one from the other sex joins your company?"

He kissed her hand, then kissed his wife next on the forehead and sat himself down beside her.

"Gertie has fallen in love!" Harrietta announced to her friend's horror.

Aubrey smiled and poured himself a cup of tea. "I hope not with that worthless husband of yours?"

"Not at all," Gertie protested. "And I would not ascribe the word 'love'—"

"Perhaps not yet," Harrietta teased.

"Who is this fortunate man?" Aubrey inquired.

"Yes! You have yet to name him. I must meet this man before I die of curiosity. Or do I know him already?"

"I think not," Gertie answered. "He left England before you were married to Vale."

"Left England? How mysterious."

"There is no sense in pursuing the matter. I am married, and nothing will come of it."

"Happiness can come of it. You may be married, but why should you be doomed to misery? Marriage has not stopped your husband from acquiring a lover."

Gertie paused, hardly daring to hope that Barclay might consider becoming her paramour.

"Who is he and when can I meet him?" Harrietta prompted.

"My dear," Aubrey interjected, "are you so sure Gertie desires for you to meet him?"

"Well, why not?" blustered Harrietta.

"As I have said, he is—he has a repute," Gertie supplied.

"But I shall not hold that against him, especially as I have yet to meet him. I profess I am predisposed to adore him if he has won the heart of my Gertie."

"He is not likely to consider me more than…than a conquest of his. And I am satisfied that our liaison be confined to the three days at the inn."

"Is that what he wishes? Did he proclaim it?"

Gertie recalled how Barclay had urged her to have no regrets, but that did not mean he wished to continue their liaison.

"No, but I think we will resume our prior association — an acquaintance of the Lowry family."

"You said he engaged you in a business proposition?"

"That is merely because his land adjoins Lowry."

This time the Marquess looked up from his tea. "Who is this?"

"He…" Gertie could not lie to Harrietta out of friendship, but she could not lie to the Marquess because he was the sort to ferret out the truth regardless. "Phineas Barclay."

Aubrey frowned.

"You know him!" Harrietta cried gleefully.

"Yes, and Gertie is right to limit her association with him."

This time it was the Marchioness who frowned. "Why?"

"He is not a man worthy of her esteem." He turned his gaze to Gertie. "I should stay far from this man."

"But why?"

"My dear, there is no mystery why he left England. He fought a duel and killed a man he had made a cuckold."

Gertie could not help rising in defense of Barclay. "Because Jonathan Weston came at him after the duel was done. Barclay only attempted to defend himself."

Aubrey paused. "That improves the light of the duel, but it does not alter my opinion of the man."

Gertie stared into her tea once more.

"I still wish to meet him!" Harrietta declared.

"He is not worth meeting, my dear."

"Do you worry that he should seduce me and make a cuckold of you?" she teased.

"Most assuredly."

"That is a fine opinion you have of my fidelity, sir!"

He smiled lovingly at her. "I will suffer your indignation for I will not have that man near my wife."

Gertie wanted to protest that Barclay did not seek to destroy marriages. Only those that were already weak drew his attention. But how could she come to the defense of a self-proclaimed debaucher?

The Marquess softened his tone as he turned to Gertie. "It is only because of the affection that I bear you that I warn you against Lord Barclay. I have known of him for many years, and nothing good ever came of consorting with him. I should not wish to see you harmed."

Gertie nodded. She trusted the Marquess not to cast his judgments lightly.

"It were best you had nothing more to do with him," Aubrey concluded.

"I indulged in a dalliance, but I am done with Lord Barclay," she assured him.

* * * * *

Her dreams, even those of her waking hours, were harder to reign in. As Gertie lay in bed, she could think of nothing but Lord Barclay. Her body tormented itself, longing for his touch, his kiss. She closed her eyes and imagined all that they had yet to do, all the ways they could explore each other's bodies. And in her heart she yearned for his presence, his company. There was no denying that she missed him—deeply.

A soft knock at her door stirred her from her bed. It was Harrietta.

"Vale can be far too stubborn at times." Harrietta sighed when the two had settled under the bedcovers together. "I attempted to reason that Barclay cannot be as bad as he deems if Gertie could tolerate him. I know no woman more sensible than you."

"Hettie, Vale is right. I trust his judgment. It takes a man to know a man."

"But you are even now sad just thinking of this Barclay!"

Gertie gave her friend a wan smile. "Yes, but a sensible woman would not be guided by feelings of sorrow. Even if I had no wish to end the liaison, why would you believe that Barclay sees me—me, of all women—differently from his other coterie?"

"Because you *are* different."

"Are you not prejudiced by your affections?"

"Then why did he kiss you? Why did he take you to his bed?"

Gertie shrugged. "Perhaps he does see me as different and wishes to satisfy his curiosity, like a patron in a confectionary sampling the many selections. Perhaps he was bored, and I was the only woman at the inn."

"He could have easily bedded a maid."

"I do not dispute that he might have even been a little intrigued by me, but I doubt that he wishes to continue our affair. What good would come of an affair?"

"Companionship, love, happiness."

"Forgive me, but those are easy answers for a woman who has found love and happiness."

"But—"

"Do not worry of me, Hettie. I have Lady Athena to keep me company."

"I told Vale that I wished to return to London with you. I did not tell him that it is because I wish to see for myself if this Barclay is as treacherous as he says."

Gertie brightened at the thought of having Harrietta back in town.

"I think the little one can travel with us," Harrietta mused aloud. "And Vale agreed to come as well. I might even persuade him to make a visit to *Madame Botreaux's*."

"I should love to have you in London! And Penelope would be quite ecstatic to see you and Vale again."

Harrietta grinned. "That place will always hold a special place in my heart. I wonder that my marriage would have turned out happily if not for *Madame Botreaux's*?"

"It would have, for you have always loved Vale and he you."

"Strange, though, how the hand of Fate works. And to think I almost did not share that wonderful place with you. When I first told Vale my idea of taking you to the *Ballroom*, he questioned the wisdom of it, but you took to it as easily as a horse to trot!"

"I do remember being aghast when you first told me."

"I remember the look upon your face! Your jaw nearly grazed the floor!"

They laughed at the memory.

"That first night Vale must have asked me a hundred times if I were certain I wished to present," Gertie recalled.

"I think he were as anxious as you. He eyed every patron who approached you."

"It was kind of him to watch over me."

"He can be far too protective."

"I was glad for it. It made me feel safe."

"I think you should grant this Hephaestus a second chance."

"Why?"

"Because he brought you pleasure. I would have your life filled with pleasure."

They talked long into the night until they both fell asleep. Harrietta did not broach the subject of Barclay too often after that, but Gertie suspected that did not mean her friend did not dwell on the matter.

Gertie stayed a happy month at Dunnesford. Though she could not stop thinking of Phineas, she felt her resolve strengthening. She would, as Aubrey suggested, cease her association with him. There was no need to keep his company. When Aubrey learned that she had ventured into St. Giles alone, he insisted on loaning his groomsman to the Lowry House twice a week. She would miss her visits to the orphan asylum with Phineas, but it was all for the best.

She became further convinced of her decision when her menses failed to show, followed by lethargy and nausea.

She was with child.

CHAPTER FIFTEEN

"AND THIS LACE—feel its intricacy—so delicate it could only be woven by the hands of children," the mercer said.

Phineas picked up the lace but allowed it to drop from his hands without much attention. He wandered to a different table to view the bolts of fabric.

"Are you ill, Phineas?" Robert inquired as he examined the lace. "You must be for I have never seen you pass up such finery."

"This silk, Lord Barclay, hails from the East. See how the golden thread shimmers in the sun?"

The mercer held up the silk. Phineas looked at the rich coloring and decided it would bring out the glow in Gertie's skin. He imagined her wearing a corset lined with the silk, her favorite riding crop in hand.

"Perhaps another day," Phineas told the mercer.

The man looked stricken. "But—but I have others coming in this afternoon. I—I told them they would be the first to follow you, the first to know what you have favored."

"Convey my condolences for it is quite a strain to have to make a decision for one's self."

Phineas reached for his hat and walked out of the shop, followed by his astonished brother.

"My word," Robert breathed, "something does ail you."

"And you detest visits to the mercer, yet you have chosen to accompany me."

"I came to thank you for your efforts with the Countess and to tell you that the papers are drawn and ready for the Lowry seal and signature. I forgot when I encountered your cheerless demeanor. Ah, perhaps a good cup of coffee will lift your spirits."

They walked by a coffee house on their way back to Phineas's apartment.

"Worry not of my spirits, Robert," Phineas advised.

"Did it take much persuasion with the Countess?"

"She is a sensible woman and immediately saw the merits of the proposal."

Robert nodded. "I noticed she must have suggested a few provisions of her own. I saw her at Hyde Park the other week—"

Phineas stopped. "You saw her?"

"Yes, is that so very odd?"

"How many days past?"

"I—perhaps a sennight—or more. Roughly a sennight."

Gertie was back in London, Phineas contemplated. She had been back for some time and had made no effort to contact him.

"Here now, why does such news upset you?"

Phineas did not answer. It was as he had feared. The regret had set in. She had allowed herself a few days indulgence but no more. He knew it would be no easy battle against her sensibility and her misplaced dedication to self-sacrifice, but he had held out hope that she had developed more tender feelings towards him and that those feelings might prove the stronger.

"Phineas, you did *not* seduce the Countess?" Robert pleaded.

He looked at his brother's fallen face.

"Oh God, you have. Damnation, Phineas!" Robert threw up his hands. "I might as well have Mr. Hancock tear up the papers for surely she will despise you when you are done with her."

"She will not jeopardize the mining venture. She is not that sort of woman."

"Then her husband surely will when he learns of this."

Phineas pressed his lips together grimly. "Alexander will not know."

"Your affairs always become public knowledge. You ought to know how servants talk."

"There were no servants," Phineas murmured. "Save for Francis."

"What the devil do you—no, no, I need no details. If you found the Countess such a sensible woman, why did you feel compelled to seduce her?"

"If you did not want her seduced, why task me with the responsibility?"

"I certainly did not urge you to lift her skirts!"

"Robert, I did not seduce her to win her approval."

Robert twisted his face in a strange form. "Then why? Because you can! Because it is your nature to attempt the dastard!"

Phineas stared into the distance, remembering his conversation with Georgina that night after Vauxhall. How was it that women could detect the truth so easily? He turned back to look at Robert, who was shaking his head as he stared at the ground. He wondered if he should deal another blow to the poor fellow.

Robert straightened. "I retract my gratitude to you!"

"I am fond of her, Robert."

The words took a moment to sink in. When they did, Phineas could see the blood drain from Robert's face.

"Of Lady Lowry?" Robert asked weakly.

"You look as if you need to sit down."

He guided his brother to a stone wall encasing a small courtyard. He remained standing while Robert sat down.

"Odd's blood, Phineas," Robert said, his mind still turning. "Why Lady Lowry?"

"The whim of Love and the cruelty of Fate."

"Cruelty?"

"That I should fall in love with a woman I cannot have."

"That has hardly stopped you before."

Yes, Phineas thought to himself, but this time it was different. This time he wanted Gertie all to himself. He certainly had no desire to share her with Alexander Farrington.

"Come," Phineas said. "I will have that cup of coffee with you, Robert, an' you will stop looking at me with such pitiful eyes."

Robert rose to his feet. "What will you intend with the Countess?"

"I know not what she intends with me. For once, I am at a loss."

Robert shook his head. "For once, I feel bloody sorry for you, Phineas."

"Pray do not. As you've discerned, we have yet to obtain the Lowry seal."

"Ah, yes," Robert remembered. "And I suppose you were due your comeuppance."

Phineas said nothing. He was not ready to concede the Countess just yet.

* * * * *

"Will you not tell Barclay?" Harrietta asked when Gertie had divulged her state. They were riding in the Dunnesford carriage to St. Giles.

"What good would come of it?" Gertie replied. "Alexander must not know that the child is not his."

"How will he not know? You and he have not…"

Gertie steeled herself. "That can be arranged."

Harrietta furrowed her brow in thought. "One could seek a physician to terminate the—"

"No! I have longed for a child for too long. I could not. But I will not have my child born a bastard. God help me, this child will not suffer from my mistake."

And she meant it. The thought of her unborn child and its future gave her the strength to carry on. After all those attempts to produce an heir, after all the different remedies Belinda had insisted on trying, she had begotten herself with child through an affair. She could have laughed in her relief—she was not barren, after all—but for her misery.

"And you think Alexander can be…seduced?" Harrietta ventured.

The prospect made Gertie cringe. "It takes but one time…"

"Oh, Gertie, there must be another way!"

"I have mulled it day and night. I have prayed for a solution to present itself."

"You could petition for a divorce. Vale will see it through Parliament. Pitt owes him a favor."

"That would happen only after a *crim con* suit. And what of the baby? What future will it have if it is born a bastard?"

Harrietta looked down at her hands.

"Come," Gertie said. "I have made you sad, and I do not wish to visit my troubles upon you. We have a number of precious girls who will be delighted to see you."

"How deucedly iniquitous this all is!" Harrietta lamented.

Gertie did not disagree, and alas, the greatest injury would fall upon an innocent babe. At times, she had imagined leaving Alexander and living an illicit life with Phineas, but always her thoughts returned to the unborn child.

"How we have missed you girls!" Gertie exclaimed as she stood with Harrietta in the *Orphan Asylum*.

"And we return bearing gifts!" the Marchioness declared as she lifted a valise. The girls clamored around Harrietta, then gasped as little white gloves trimmed with lace emerged.

Gertie smiled as their eyes widened into saucers. She felt a tap upon her shoulder and turned to find Mr. Winters at her elbow.

"Your ladyship, there is a matter that must needs be addressed to you," he informed her. "If you would come with me into my study…"

She followed him readily, wondering what he could be alluding to.

"How is Peggy?" she asked, fearing he meant to reveal some bad news about the babe.

"Good, good," he replied. "You will find she has put on more flesh since last you saw her."

"How wonderful!" she sighed, but she noted Mr. Winters appeared uncomfortable still.

He opened the door of his study to allow her entry. "You have a guest, Lady Lowry."

She saw him only after she had stepped into the room. Even in the dimness, one could not mistake the form of Phineas Barclay. She turned back to Mr. Winters, but the man had closed the door behind him, leaving her alone with Barclay. Her heart throbbed painfully as if her chest were too small a cavity for it.

"I had to ask Mr. Winters when he expected you for you would not return my letters," he explained.

The traitor, she thought to herself as she glared at the door.

"I have been visiting my friend at Dunnesford," she reminded him.

"You returned over a fortnight ago."

His grimness surprised her. His letters, though curt in their request for her audience, had surprised her as well. She had convinced herself that he would want nothing to do with her upon their return to London. Perhaps he had wished to speak of her regarding the copper mining, though the papers had all been signed and the digging had begun.

"I have been busy," she answered. "And rather fatigued."

His expression eased and he took a step towards her. "Are you well, Gertie?"

The concern in his voice made the breath catch in her throat. She turned away from him. She was *not* well. She was terrible. Ever since she had discovered her pregnancy, she had been plagued by sleepless nights. She glanced into Barclay's searching eyes. The tenderness reflected in those radiant eyes was an arrow through her heart. Suddenly she wanted to tell him everything, to feel his comforting arms about her. But that would not do. It was best to believe the worst where Lord Barclay was concerned.

"I am well enough," she replied, her mouth dry. She walked towards the bookcase on the other side of the room from him and pretended to review the book spines. "Did you wish to speak to me of the mine? I understand it is going well?"

"I wished to know how you fared," he said.

Her stomach twisted, but she forced a nonchalant shrug as she turned to him. "Now you know."

His gaze narrowed at her. "I see. I was mistaken about our time at the inn, then."

She raised her brows. "Your pardon? What is there to mistake?"

A muscle rippled along his jaw. He stepped towards her.

"Though I did fear that you would repent our time," he continued.

"Nay, I do not repent it," she said with forced gaiety, "but what more needs to be addressed? We amused ourselves, you and I, but one could hardly expect the affair to continue?"

He was still advancing towards her, so she turned to leave, but his arm blocked her path, trapping her between the bookcase and his body.

"Amused ourselves?" he echoed. "Is that how you see our time together?"

Her heart thumped furiously. "La, sir, how else would one see it? You of all people should understand."

"It meant more to me than mere amusement."

Gertie shut her eyes. If she looked into his gaze, her armor would crack and she would find herself a crumpled heap at his feet.

His statement hurt more than anything. It was the last thing she wanted to hear him say. She would have done better had he confessed that he had taken her to bed in error.

"Gertie…"

She felt her legs tremble beneath her at the caress of her name.

He leaned in towards her. "I counted the days until we would meet."

Her eyes flew open. "I am a married woman."

"That did not stop you at the inn."

"Things have changed."

He straightened, and she took that opportunity to escape from him. She leaned over the writing desk for support.

"You have had a change of heart," he noted.

She nodded. He grasped both her arms and turned her to him.

"I don't believe it," he said.

"You may—you may disbelieve all you wish. It does not change my situation."

His nearness consumed the breathable air about her. She had to put some distance between them.

"I can change it. What do you wish of me? I will grant it."

She shook her head. "You cannot. Nor do I wish you to."

"Gertie!"

For the first time she heard the desperation.

"I think it best," she said with a trembling voice, "that you not seek my audience anymore."

"Why? I would be the Cicisbeo to you and demand naught from you."

"But I do not wish it."

His grasp tightened about her arms. Her head was beginning to spin.

"Gertie, if you knew the depths of my affection—"

She shook her head violently. "Cease! I wish to hear no more. I wish for you not to trouble me! I wish not to see you!"

With a cry, she wrenched herself free. She yanked open the

door and fled out of the room. Despite the tears clouding her eyes, she made her way out into the yard behind the asylum. Beneath an elm tree, she sobbed as her heart broke in twain.

CHAPTER SIXTEEN

"**P**HINEAS? PHINEAS!"

Phineas looked over his tea at Georgina, who had invited herself over in hopes of coaxing him to attend her on her visit to the milliner.

"Phineas, you are not yourself," his sister said, biting into a crumpet. "Robert had said as much but I could hardly believe it. What can possibly ruffle our dear brother?"

He made no response. His mind still dwelled in the orphan asylum and his last exchange with Gertie. She had stunned him. He who had never been for a loss of words had been rendered speechless. He had expected some resistance from her, but her vehemence had disconcerted him. Still, he was not ready to submit to her professed wish. There had to be a way to win her over, but he was at a loss over how.

"I require your services," Georgina continued, "for I insist on being properly dressed if I am to give testimony at the *crim con.* Rather, I wish to shine beautifully."

Phineas put down his tea. Perhaps there was a way to Gertie through Lady Athena…

Gibbons entered the room. "Lord Barclay, a lady is here to see you."

Phineas leaped to his feet. The Countess! At last! She had realized her affection for him. But the woman waiting for him in the hall was not Gertie. Despite the veil covering her face, he could tell from her form it was not whom he desired. Her *robe l'anglaise* fitted her petite frame too smartly.

"May we speak in private, Lord Barclay?" the woman asked.

"I have never denied a woman a request for privacy," Barclay returned, though he sensed a foreboding tenor to the prospect. He showed her into his study. "May I offer you—"

She shook her head. "I will not be long."

Standing by his writing table, he waited for her to begin. She lifted her veil to reveal young, soft features, a pleasing but not extraordinary countenance with high cheekbones, thick eyebrows, and small lips. He did not recognize her physiognomy, but she revealed herself soon enough.

"Gertie must not know that I came to see you."

He bowed. "You must be the Marchioness of Dunnesford."

She appraised him from head to foot and seemed somewhat impressed.

"To what do I owe the pleasure?" he asked.

She hesitated. "Gertie knows not that I am here, but she told me everything. About you. And her."

"Indeed," he said, unimpressed. He knew the affection Gertie bore the Marchioness, but if the Lady Aubrey were such a good friend, why was she here?

His tone must have surprised her for she elaborated, "Gertie is my dearest friend. I will not see her harmed."

"Ah, the lioness has come to threaten the wolf to keep his distance. I am glad that Gertie—Lady Lowry—has at least one protector."

"Yes, but…"

"You need not have wasted your time, my lady."

He made a movement to show her out the door.

"It pains me to see her in such despair," she insisted. "And if you care for her as much as I, you will not wish to cause her more grief."

He looked at her sharply. "Madam, I would disavow my soul to ease her suffering. But you will be relieved to know that she has already sworn off further association with me."

The Marchioness winced. "I know. She told me of her dialogue with you at the orphan asylum. But I think—I suspect you are not the sort of man to give up easily. And you must understand that the more you pursue her, the more she is pained."

"I have no intention of making a public spectacle if that is what you fear. If she has entrusted you with her confidence, then there is but the three of us who have any knowledge of what occurred."

"That is not what I meant. You do not understand..."

He raised his brows, feeling his patience wearing thin as the last memory of Gertie brought back the pain of her words.

"Lady Lowry would have me believe that my presence is loathsome to her," he said. "You will not convince me where she has failed. Lady Lowry—Gertie has a perturbing affinity for the martyr. I intend to persuade her from it."

"You must not!"

His irritation rose. Though he knew the Marchioness to act out of her love for Gertie, he did not appreciate her meddling. "I think the one who fails to understand is you."

She had a tortured look on her face. "Please cease your efforts where Gertie is concerned."

"Madam, I think there is no more that needs be discussed."

He headed for the door with every intention of having Gibbons escort her out. He could have provided her a set-down for her interference, but only the knowledge of her friendship with Gertie stayed him from making any biting remarks.

"She is with child."

His hand felt heavy upon the handle of the door as the words sunk in.

"Your child," Lady Aubrey added.

With slow deliberation, he turned to face her. She looked ready to cry.

"Are you certain?" he asked, his voice near a whisper.

"Certain she is with child or certain it is yours?"

Needing time to think, he walked away from the door towards the window.

"She is certain," she said. "Of both."

"Does Alexander know?"

"He knows nothing. And he will not have reason to believe the child not to be his."

The realization began to sink in. No wonder Gertie had rebuffed him with such passion.

"So you see that it is fruitless to seek her out," Lady Aubrey stated.

He put a hand to the back of his neck. The world had shifted beneath his feet. All the thoughts and hopes he had harbored were no longer germane. The Cruelty of Fate.

"She will not endanger the future of her child."

"I know," he acknowledged. He knew what this child meant to Gertie. He spoke, but his voice reached his ears as if emanating from someone else. "Nor would I ask her to."

The Marchioness released an audible sigh. She walked over and put a hand upon his arm.

"You are a good man. I suspected as much, for Gertie would not have fallen in love with a man who was not."

He nearly choked and could not help a grimace as he looked down at the Marchioness. "But not enough to wish to be with me."

"You must not think thusly. I wish with all my heart that she could have both you and the child. She deserves so much more happiness than she has had."

He took a deep breath, but it only made his chest ache.

"I can see that you love her."

He winced and said with some bitterness. "That does not matter now."

"It always matters."

A sentimental and womanly statement, he thought dismissively.

"If it would have made Gertie happy, I would have professed it to the world," he said. "But as such, it shall remain locked in my bosom."

Feeling the weight of sadness, he glanced down at his hands. "I take it that I am not to know this child of mine?" he asked.

"Alas…" She replaced the veil over her face. "I should depart. If I could…if you should ever require anything of me, Lord Barclay, I would be only too glad to be of service."

He grasped her hand before she could leave. "If you find an opportunity, if you could convey—tell Gertie I wish her well. I wish her all the happiness she can find."

The Marchioness nodded. She sauntered to the door and left without further word. Phineas stared at the floor, the rug upon it a colorful blur before his eyes. A range of emotions—anger, despair, and sorrow— threatened to assault him. How dare Gertie try to keep this child from him? How dare she sacrifice her own happiness for this child? How dare she allow Alexander to believe the child to be his own?

The last thought made the hairs on his neck stand on end. But with his outrage came compassion and sympathy for what Gertie endured. As he recalled their last exchange, he realized her pain. He had been too taken aback by her rejection at the time to recognize how much she suffered. The grief hung heavy upon his heart as he thought of her agony, but she had a consolation—a child that she could love. He had nothing.

"Phineas?"

He looked up to see Georgina standing at the door. He must have looked a sorry sight for she hurried to his side.

"Phineas, who was that woman? What did she have to say to you?"

"I had but met her acquaintance today."

"And who is she?"

"I will not reveal her." He straightened and faced his sister. "Come, did you not to intend to seek my company to the milliner?"

She eyed him skeptically.

"One must always look her best in a *crim con* suit, eh?" he prodded.

Georgina agreed and they set off for the shops in Mayfair, but it proved a futile distraction. He could not stop thinking of Gertie and how she was now forever lost to him.

CHAPTER SEVENTEEN

G ERTIE WATCHED AS the serving maid poured the burgundy into Alexander's glass. It was one of the finest bottles she could procure, and she expected that Alexander would take to it favorably.

"The Herrefords have an heir—two, in fact, as Lady Herreford produced twins," Belinda remarked over dinner.

Alexander scowled and reached for the wine. Gertie kept her gaze to her soup.

"And they have been wed but a year," Belinda added. "I wonder if you should consult a physician, Alexander?"

It had been the first time the Dowager Lowry had contemplated the possibility that the lack of an offspring might be attributable to her son.

"He must first need plow the right field," Sarah muttered as she watched her soup sliding off the spoon.

Alexander glared at his sister. Sarah responded with a defiant look.

"I beg your pardon?" Belinda asked.

"I have no wish to marry Mr. Rowland," Sarah declared.

By the look in her sister-in-law's eyes, Gertie realized what her sister intended to employ.

"No one else has asked for your hand," Alexander responded evenly.

"Because you have discouraged them all!"

"Mr. Rowland is a good prospect," Belinda defended.

Sarah grimaced. "I bear him no affection! I loathe his presence!"

"He will care for you well," Alexander said. "I have no wish to discuss this further. The matter is settled."

"You care only that he has money that you might lavish your

mistress with gifts!"

Alexander became livid as Belinda's eyes grew wide.

"Mistress?" Belinda echoed.

"He has entertained her for nearly a six-month," Sarah supplied. "Lowry has no heir because Alexander has been sowing his seed elsewhere."

The nostrils of the Dowager flared. She turned to Alexander, who finished off his glass.

"You would bring such disgrace upon our family?" Belinda demanded. Gertie had never seen her in such a state of anger. "Have you no shame? No regard for the Lowry name?"

Alexander poured himself another glass. "It is of no significance."

"No significance? You would leave Lowry without an heir? Do you realize who shall rule over us if you should die? Your duty–"

"I know my duty."

"This is unacceptable. Who is this strumpet?" Belinda turned to her daughter. "How long have you known of this and not spoken of it to me?"

Sarah avoided her gaze.

Belinda turned her accusatory glare at Gertie. "Have you known all this time?"

"Lowry will have an heir," Alexander stated. "If you but possessed a little patience, mother…"

"Patience? It has been three years. I have been naught but patient! And to think how much effort I have expended to assist the family—how much it tries my nerves to think our future has not been secured—yet you deliberately deny me ease of mind."

An uneasy silence descended over the dinner table. Alexander ground his teeth and poured himself more of the wine.

The dinner could not end soon enough, but Gertie was satisfied that Alexander had consumed more than half the bottle. After dinner, he secluded himself in his study. Gertie sighed with relief for if he had taken himself to Blake's, who knew when he might return. She sat in her bedchambers, waiting for Alexander's footsteps in the hall. She would open her door as he entered his chambers and invite him into her bed.

But when she finally heard his footsteps, she found herself

without the will.

"Come along, Gertie," she coaxed herself. "It will be no different than before."

Which was a lie, for Phineas Barclay had changed everything. How she missed him! She had not seen or heard from him since she last saw him at the orphan asylum.

The child. Her unborn child. She placed a hand to her belly. Finding resolve, she rose to her feet. The door to her chambers swung open then, and in its frame stood her husband. From the glassy look in his eyes, she surmised that he had had more to drink. Wordlessly she waited for him to approach, her heart quickening but not from anticipation. He staggered towards her.

She closed her eyes as he kissed her, slobbering over her face. Even when he hadn't been inebriated, his kisses could not compare to those of Barclay. She tried her best not to push him away and allowed him to stumble her into her bed. He fell on top of her and began pulling up her skirts. Closing her eyes, she turned to her memories of Barclay in an attempt to transport herself away from the moment. How her body had craved for his touch and all the wonderful ways he could make her feel...There would never be another like him.

Her eyes flew open upon feeling penetration. Above her, Alexander grunted and huffed as if from arduous exertion. Her saving grace was that it did not take Alexander long to finish. He collapsed on top of her. She pushed him off. She reached under her bed to pull out the chamber pot and retched.

* * * * *

The Dowager Lowry hummed as she worked upon her embroidery in the drawing room. Gertie noticed Belinda had been in good spirits ever since Gertie had announced that her menses had not come. She had waited only a sennight after that first night with Alexander. As soon as she had made her announcement, he had ceased to visit her bedchambers. Gertie hoped that he had retained his mistress over his mother's objections for she wanted no more of his attentions.

"As I shall have more money than matter to spend it upon, I

think I shall choose the most expensive of gowns," Sarah declared as she sullenly leafed through a collection of wedding gown plates.

Gertie, knitting a cap for the baby, said nothing. She felt sorry for Sarah, but her sister-in-law's despondency and self-pity had made her more cross with Gertie.

The butler entered the room to state that a Mrs. Georgina Westmoreland was here to see Lady Lowry.

"Absolutely not," Belinda replied. "Who does that woman presume she is coming into a respectable household?"

"I will see her," Gertie declared, drawing gasps from the two other women.

"You will not allow that woman another moment in our house."

Gertie gazed at Belinda without uncertainty. A calm had come over her in the last sennight. It was as if the strength of Lady Athena had finally seeped into the bones of Gertie Farrington.

Turning to the butler, Gertie said, "You may show her into the library."

Belinda and Sarah let loose a cacophony of protests, but Gertie left the drawing room without addressing them. She, and not they, was the Countess of Lowry.

"Our tea will be served shortly. Will you partake?" Gertie asked as she entered the library.

Georgina turned and smiled, and Gertie was reminded instantly of Phineas. The brother and sister shared the same disarming smile.

"Thank you, no," Georgina replied. "You are kind—as you were that day I met you—to grant me an audience."

"Will you not sit?" Gertie gestured to a sofa.

Georgina obliged. "You will think me forward in coming to you. You do not know me well, and our families have not been the best of friends."

"I harbor no ill will towards the Barclays," Gertie assured her as she, too, sat down.

Georgina nodded. "In truth, I know not what good will come of my speaking with you. I only know that I feel compelled by my love for my brother."

"How fares the Baron?"

Georgina colored. "My other brother—Phineas."

Gertie took a deep breath. Of course Georgina had meant Phineas. All the same, she had hoped it would not be.

"How is Lord Barclay?" Gertie rephrased politely.

Georgina stared. "Do you not know? He is misery itself."

Gertie felt herself grow pale. "Indeed? I'm sorry to hear it."

Her curt reply seemed to surprise Georgina.

"Phineas would not explain much to me," Georgina said, "but he need not have."

Gertie rose to her feet and turned away. She could feel Georgina's stare upon her and wondered what the woman knew.

"You could do much to ease his pain."

"I doubt it," Gertie replied, grateful her voice did not tremble as much as her insides. "I have not heard from him in over a fortnight."

"That is because he has taken himself to Bath to nurse his grief. And he detests Bath."

Gertie felt her heart breaking once more. She had allowed her own misery to consume her, not thinking it was possible that he suffered as well. The thought of his agony was too much.

"I know not what your brother has told you," Gertie said, "but I think you must have misunderstood him."

"I understand him to be deeply in love with you."

Gertie nearly choked on her breath. The tears pressed hard against the back of her eyes.

"Are you not in love with him?" Georgina asked quietly.

"It matters not," Gertie replied weakly.

"I would not recommend any woman to suffer what I have, but the laws can be a remedy."

Gertie shook her head. "Our situations differ."

"Lady Lowry, I know you little, but what I have seen, pleases me. And I think that you are not without sorrow in the absence of my brother. I would see both of you happy."

"As would I," Gertie relented. "And I have considered it many, many times. But it were not possible. Not for us. I think Phin—your brother will forget me soon enough."

"I think not. He may have taken many a woman to bed on whim, but love—love he takes not lightly."

"He did not pursue me afterwards with much effort," Gertie

said with a touch of bitterness as she recalled how easily Barclay had capitulated to her demands. She had expected him to make at least one or two attempts to convince her otherwise. Apparently, it had been rather easy for him to give her up.

"Yes, which is unlike him, such that I think it can only be the greatness of his love and respect for you that he has not."

"Mrs. Westmoreland, you are a romantic."

"A trait I inherited from my father. You would not think it for he, as well as my mother, had reputations as libertines and debauchers. But my father was madly in love with my mother. After she passed, I think he was beside himself, attempting to erase the memory of her through the companionship of others."

Gertie remembered well what Phineas had shared regarding his father. She remembered every moment with Phineas.

"Mrs. Westmoreland," Gertie began.

"Pray address me as Georgina. I shall not be Mrs. Westmoreland for long."

"I commend you for your devotion to your brother, but if you understood my state—you see, I am expecting a child and I am resolved to be happy in my marriage and my new…situation."

The revelation drew a gasp from Georgina, who knitted her brows in thought.

"It is useless to persuade me otherwise," Gertie finished, her tone unwavering though she felt like crumbling inside.

"I did not know—much felicitation to you and your family."

Gertie smiled wanly. "You are welcome to stay for tea."

"I wonder that the Lady Dowager and Lady Sarah would welcome me?"

"You are my guest," Gertie insisted.

"Thank you, but I shall not trouble you further."

Georgina rose to her feet and headed towards the door. She hesitated, then glanced back at Gertie. "I do hope you achieve the happiness you desire, Lady Lowry."

Gertie could not move herself to walk Georgina out. She could see herself becoming friends with Georgina, but Mrs. Westmoreland had the most imploring eyes—eyes that could wear down her resolve. It was best not to foster relationships that would only ignite painful memories. She had made her decision, and there was no turning back.

Chapter Eighteen

"T HE BIGGEST LOAD of copper we have ever come across," Robert was saying. "Why, it shall sustain our mines for years to come!"

Phineas, reviewing the clothes his valet had laid out upon his bed, listened with half an ear. He picked up a silk waistcoat and tossed it aside onto a chair.

"I have been speaking with Mr. Wempole, a banker here in London, to finance improvements to our smelting house," Robert continued. "I should dearly like for you to be part of the discussion."

"Robert, you know that I am in London but a few days. Once I have dispensed of my properties here, including this apartment, I am taking Prudence to Scotland."

Robert shook his head. "I think you shall enjoy Scotland as much as you enjoy Bath."

"Nevertheless, Prudence wishes to see the lakes of Scotland. Did you know she is quite the poetess? I am sure the landscape will inspire her pen."

"And since when did you take in interest in our little sister?"

"A young woman should not be confined to lessons in French and dance alone. There is more to the world than Lowry—or even London."

"And you intend to learn her the other worlds?"

"I have no intention of corrupting her if that is what you fear, but I intend that she learn more of human nature than what is taught by her governess and tutor."

"No, no, I think it splendid that you will be playing the father to Prudence. I said as much to my wife when she voiced concerns."

Phineas smiled. "Did you indeed? I knew you would grow into

the role of the Baron in time."

"But I've no skill at negotiating. Will you not meet with Mr. Wempole? He will be at the Bennington soiree tonight."

Phineas paused, the memory of the Bennington ball pressing on his conscience. "Robert, I trust your abilities."

"Georgina may be there tonight, and she would be delighted to see you. I take it you received her letter regarding her successful petition for divorce?"

"And happily ensconced with her lover now."

"Yes, well, I have not decided whether I like the fellow, but he cannot be nearly as bad as those that Abigail has entertained."

"I shall pay Georgina a visit on mine own. I have no interest in attending a soiree."

Phineas returned to examining which of his attire he wished to pack for the trip.

"If you would but accompany me at this one meeting—to ensure the discussion starts off properly, I think that would leave me with greater confidence to finish the matter."

"And why do you think I should prove persuasive with this Mr. Wempole? I am no favorite among men."

"Have you seduced his wife before?"

"What does she look like?"

"It is unlikely. She is near sixty in age and has the gout."

"Robert—"

"Surely you do not intend to evade all the places where you and the Countess…"

Phineas looked sharply at his brother.

"Georgina told me…you cannot fear crossing her path."

"Fear?" Phineas echoed. He longed for the sight of her. Even in Bath, when he knew it to be impossible, he would round the street corner thinking how marvelous it would be if he should come across her. It was true he left London for he could not bear seeing her and knowing he could not have her. But escaping London provided no relief. The memory of her plagued him everywhere.

But he had assured the Marchioness of Dunnesford that he would cause no pain to Gertie. How he had longed to write to Gertie, to ask after her and hear how she fared. He contemplated if they could be friends for he missed her company as much as he missed her body, but such notions were beyond foolishness for a man of his understanding.

"I should not have spoken," Robert apologized.

"One meeting," Phineas said. "And that is the last concession you will wrest from me."

He picked up a waistcoat he had had worn at that little posting inn where his life had changed, fingering the fabric as if he could feel her essence upon it. He knew that time would heal his broken heart, and a small part of him wished that his heart might never heal completely. He never once regretted his love for Gertie, and there was a bit of satisfaction that he could help bring about that which she had longed for, that which would make her happy. Beyond anything, he wanted for her the greatest of happiness.

* * * * *

"I feel better," Gertie responded to Harrietta's question as they strolled arm in arm down one of the allées of the Bennington property. "The lethargy is much improved, and it is a relief to be able to leave the house."

Also a relief was the lack of attention from Alexander once it became known that she was pregnant. She suspected that he had taken up once more with his mistress, for which she was glad. The Dowager paid little attention to her son for her supreme wish—that of an heir—had been satisfied. Her next project was ensuring that Sarah married Mr. Rowland in a wedding ceremony that would be the talk of London for years to come.

"I can hardly believe how much I have had to loosen my stays," Gertie commented. "I remember with you, the evidence that you were carrying was not visible until two months before the babe came!"

"I thank you for your overstatement, but the blush of motherhood never sat upon me quite as lovely as it does you," Harrietta returned.

Gertie placed a hand to her belly. "I am in love with her already."

"Convinced of a daughter?"

"I cannot attest to why, but I am nearly certain it is. Perhaps it is merely my hopes. I had always wished for a little sister growing up. A daughter would be perfect."

Somehow, she felt that Phineas would have been glad of a daughter. She rarely thought of the babe without thinking of Phineas. How bittersweet life could be!

"The Dowager Lowry would be devastated," Harrietta grinned.

"And Alexander beyond disappointed, but, Hettie, I no longer care what they should think."

Harrietta squeezed her arm proudly. "Shall we see no more of Lady Athena for a spell?"

"Aye, I know not that Lady Athena shall return to *The Ballroom*, but I shall always have a special place in my heart for her."

"I can hardly wait for the babe to arrive. I know our children will become the best of friends. It grows dark. Shall we return to the house?"

They turned and headed back towards the house.

"Do you suppose," Gertie began after a moment of silence. "Do you suppose it would be awkward if I inquired from the Benningtons if they had word of Phineas—Lord Barclay?"

"Do you wish that he had communicated with you?" Harrietta asked sharply.

"Yes. And no. It would have broken my heart anew each time I heard from him. And yet, I wonder that he could sever me from consideration so easily?"

"I doubt he did that. You were quite persuasive when last you spoke."

"Yes, but...I had expected that he would not have capitulated so easily lest his affections for me were less than profound."

Harrietta bit her lower lip. "Does it matter to you his affection for you?"

"It should not alter the outcome, but it pains me to think that he did not care enough to attempt more than he did. I believe him to be the sort of man that allows no obstacle in the pursuit of his objective—certainly not where the fair sex is concerned."

"Gertie, I..."

"I know there is little evidence to sustain my belief outside his seductions, but I felt it when I was with him. I suppose I had suffered many delusions where he is concerned."

"You did not," Harrietta said with a heavy sigh. "Gertie, you may not forgive me once you hear what I am to say, but I hope you will know that I acted out of my love for you."

Puzzled, Gertie stared at her friend.

"After you had—after our visit to the orphan asylum," Harrietta unfolded, "I went to see Lord Barclay. It broke my heart to see you in such pain. And I suspected, as you did, that he might not relent so easily. When I had spoken with him, it was clear to me that he would not leave you alone. I revealed—I revealed that you were with child."

Gertie stopped in her tracks and allowed Harrietta's arm to slip from hers. "He knows?"

Harrietta nodded. "And I think that is the sole reason he ceased his pursuit of you. And I could tell it was no easy agreement for him. If ever a man loved with all his heart, it was—is Lord Barclay."

"Pardon me, madam, but did you speak the name of Barclay?"

The two women turned to find one of the guests, an Army officer dressed in full regimentals, at their elbow. Harrietta glanced at Gertie, but neither recognized the man.

"Who wishes to know?" Harrietta asked.

The man bowed. "Major Summers, your servant, my ladies."

"There are any number of Barclays," Gertie supplied.

"I seek Phineas Barclay, a man who was assumed dead at one time."

"Are you an acquaintance of his?"

"I should like to be."

The edge in the man's voice gave Gertie pause. There was a look in his eye that she did not trust.

She shrugged, "Alas, I think the last we heard he was in Bath."

"But you are acquaintances, or friends, of his?" Major Summers pressed.

"My husband's family is a distant relation of the Barclays. We are not close. If you would excuse us, we have a need to visit the powdering room."

Though the man had another question on his tongue, they swept past him before he could utter a word.

"I wonder what he wanted of Phineas?" Gertie questioned aloud.

"Do you despise me?" Harrietta asked.

Gertie studied the aggrieved face of her best friend. She threw her arms about Harrietta. "Never! Never could I despise you. But I wonder that you did not speak to me sooner?"

"I am a silly fool," Harrietta laughed shakily.

"You are indeed, Lady Dunnesford!"

Harrietta returned the embrace. "Come, let us to the card tables. I will let you win at piquet."

"Are you so assured I would lose?"

"After my first foray into cards, I vowed to be as adept as I could!"

Gertie nodded, knowing the story behind the Marchioness and how she once found herself in debt to the wrong person. "I will need the winnings as I am sure Alexander will have been at dice for quite some time tonight!"

They walked, arm in arm once more, to the card room. Gertie felt her thoughts swirling about her head like churning butter. She had a dozen questions she wished to ask of Harrietta, but they would have to wait until they could talk in greater privacy. Her tread felt lighter to think that perhaps it had not been such an easy thing for Phineas to give up on her. Phineas, Phineas, Phineas. She hoped he knew that it had not been easy for her to forsake him.

And then she felt Harrietta stiffen. She looked up and felt the blood drain from her. It was as if her thoughts were toying with her vision, mocking her with the mirage of her memories. For there stood Phineas Barclay, as gloriously dressed as was his custom. The only aspect that made her question if he might not be an illusion after all were the dark crescents beneath his eyes and the whiteness about his lips when he caught her gaze. It seemed her heart threatened to beat out of her chest. She could move no limb. She could only stare, blinking, expecting him to disappear at any moment. But he did not. He stood as frozen as she.

"I—I think I shall see if Vale wishes to join us in a round of whist," Harrietta mumbled before scurrying into the card room.

"I shall ask for our horses," Robert Barclay said.

Gertie had not even noticed the presence of the baron, but she knew that she now stood alone with Barclay. He spoke first.

"Gertie."

The simple utterance, nearly a whisper upon his lips, told her that all that Harrietta had said was true. It was at once a caress and a tribute to time passed.

He straightened and his tone became more formal. He bowed. "Countess, what an unexpected pleasure. I hope you are well?"

His eyes searched her. She felt a lump growing in her throat. Nodding, she replied, "And you? You have been well?"

He nodded. The silence of embarrassment over their mutual lies fell upon them.

"I heard you had been in Bath," Gertie said at last.

"And I leave for Scotland in a few days. From there…perhaps I shall travel to the Continent once more—Italy or Greece. I am sure to have a different perspective if I am there of mine own choosing."

The thought of him so far away wrenched her heart, but what did she expect?

"Good tidings to you in your travels then," Gertie said, the words sounding exceedingly lame in her own ears.

A muscle twitched along his jaw, and the pain in his eyes was like a stab into the deepest part of her. There was much more to be said, much more she wished to speak to him, but the words would not emerge.

"Felicitations to you—and to your family. I pray that you are happy, Gertie."

She shut her eyes to keep back the tears. *Ye Gods*, she cried silently. She wanted to crumble to the floor. The weight of their collective misery was too much to bear.

"That is him," a voice behind her said.

She opened her eyes to see Major Summers striding up to Barclay. He was trembling with rage.

"Lord Barclay," Summers called out, "If you are a man, I demand satisfaction!"

Barclay assessed the man with cool eyes.

"And if I am not?" he returned blandly.

That had the effect of making the Major more furious.

"Then you, sir, are a coward!"

Gertie saw Phineas' nostrils flare ever so slightly.

"I have been called far worse."

"Will you or will you not be a man?" Summers demanded.

"My dear fellow," Barclay said, retrieving his snuff box and flicking it open, "who the devil are you and why such an interest in my manhood?"

Summers straightened in an attempt to match Barclay's height. "I am Major Summers, aide-de-camp to the Duke of York, and you, sir, owe me satisfaction."

Gertie felt her stomach plummet. The man would not relent. His escalating volume was beginning to draw curious onlookers from the card room.

"I know you not; therefore, I cannot possibly be in debt to you," Barclay returned as he inhaled a pinch of snuff.

"You know my wife," Summers ground out between clenched teeth.

Gertie saw a faint flicker of recognition in Barclay's eyes.

"Yes, I made her acquaintance at Vauxhall when she was with that fellow over there. Have you called him out as well?"

Gertie looked to see a young sergeant standing near.

"He did not attempt to seduce my wife!" fumed Summers,

"You have no evidence I attempted any such thing."

"I had it all from the servants. They told me how you had suggested she spend some days at her sister's house when her sister was conveniently absent. It was during a week when I was in Kent. I remember it well for it rained exceptionally hard for three days' time."

Gertie snapped to attention. The friend that Barclay had intended to see before he came upon her and her chaise …must have been the Major's wife.

"I know your reputation," Summers continued. "I think many a husband would applaud me if I put a bullet through your head."

"I would not disagree with your statement."

"I demand satisfaction!" Summers cried, no longer able to endure being toyed with.

"And why should I give it?" Phineas asked haughtily as he took another pinch of snuff.

Summers looked ready to explode. "Will you be a coward then? Have you no honor?"

"In general, none."

Summers took off his glove and threw it at Phineas. The glove knocked the contents of the snuff box onto Phineas and grazed his chin before falling to the floor.

Barclay brushed the snuff off his waistcoat and calmly returned the snuff box to his pocket. "Swords or pistols?"

"No!" Gertie gasped. She turned to the Major. "You are mistaken. Your wife is mistaken."

"I believe the choice to be yours," the Major sneered, ignoring her.

"I assure you I am equally comfortable with both," Phineas said.

Summers stiffened. "Pistols then. Name your seconds."

"Phineas!" exclaimed Robert, who had just returned.

Gertie did not notice him or any of the others that had gathered about them. She put her hand on the Major. "You are mistaken. You do not understand."

"Madam, this is none of your affair!" Summers barked.

"My brother Robert shall be one," Phineas replied.

Having no luck with Summers, Gertie turned to Barclay. "What are you doing?! Surely you are jesting…"

But he did not look at her. He kept his gaze upon Summers. A shiver went through her as she glimpsed the determination in Barclay's eyes.

"Phineas, this is madness!" Robert cried. "Do you not remember that if you fight another duel–"

"I remember," Phineas said brusquely.

"My seconds will inform yours of the time and place," Summers said.

Phineas bowed. "I await our assignation."

"No!" Gertie cried again, this time loud enough to command the attention of both men. "You will not fight this unnecessary duel."

She turned to Summers, her hands clenched to contain her trembling. "You are mistaken. Lord Barclay was never with your wife—because he was with me. We—"

Phineas cut her off. "Gertie, no."

He turned to Summers. "She knows not what she speaks. I will meet you where and when you wish."

"He never had the opportunity to seduce your wife," Gertie

persisted. "We spent those three days, Lord Barclay and I, at the Four Horse Posting Inn. You may ask any who worked at the inn and they will attest to it."

She looked to Phineas, who was shaking his head.

"She is a fool," Phineas said to Summers. "She hopes to save my life by sacrificing her honor. But mine is not a life worth saving. Lady Lowry suffers delusions of grandeur."

"I may be a fool," Gertie returned, "but I suffer no delusions. I would not forget those three days with you for the world."

Phineas closed his eyes for a moment. When he opened them, she thought she saw tears.

"It is not too late to retract," he said to her. "Remember—you have much to live for."

She shook her head. "Not without you."

Phineas turned to Summers. "She fancies herself in love with me. Surely you can see that she is not of sound mind at present."

But Summers had a strange look upon his face as he glanced between Barclay and Gertie.

"Yes, I fancy myself in love with you," Gertie stated, feeling an odd sense of freedom as she spoke. "Will you disavow you feel the same?"

"For God's sake, say you love her!" Robert exclaimed. "You know you do!"

"Robert, if you speak another word, I shall kill you 'an the Major leaves me standing," Phineas said.

Emboldened, Gertie took a step towards him. "Will you dare deny that you love me?"

His voice was hoarse, but he replied. "I would deny it to my death, Lady Lowry."

Gertie smiled as the tears rolled down her cheek. "You are ever the man that I love and more."

It would be hard to put into words the look in his eyes, but she knew he loved her. And for the moment, the weight of sorrow that she had carried was lifted from her. Her heart was a caged bird set free, and it soared with joy.

"The Four Horse Inn, you say?" Summers interrupted.

Gertie nodded. This time Phineas did not refute her.

"It appears I was mistaken, sir," Summers said to Barclay. He gave a curt bow. "Please accept my apologies."

Grumbling to himself, he stalked away with his sergeant.

Gertie let out the breath she had been holding. Turning to Phineas, she curled her lips in a small and shaky smile. It was not until now that she realized the large crowd that had assembled around them, but she did not care that the world knew of her love for this man.

But from the corner of her eye, she saw Alexander approaching.

CHAPTER NINETEEN

YOU *ARE EVER the man that I love.* The music of angels could not have been more melodious to his ears. Phineas stared at Gertie, her face bright with tears and full of love. He wanted nothing more than to crush her in his embrace and show her that his love could compare to hers. Was it possible to feel something greater than joy? He would have covered the distance between them and taken her in his arms, but a movement from the crowd stalled him.

He watched as Alexander approached, and he readied himself for what was likely to be his second challenge of the evening, but Alexander turned to face Gertie.

"Whore," Alexander spat.

He pulled his arm back and struck her. She fell to the ground.

Phineas leaped towards Alexander but someone stepped in front of him and held him in place. He fought against the arms that held him.

"Unhand me!" he demanded. "I will throttle that bloody coward within an inch of his life!"

He heard his brother call his name, but his attention was pinned on Alexander. He would wring the little bastard's neck…

"Touch her again and I will claw your eyes out!" the Marchioness cried to Alexander as she hovered over Gertie.

"Damn you! Unhand me!" Phineas growled as he felt himself being dragged away.

"Lord Lowry, I cannot tolerate such displays in my house," Mr. Bennington admonished. "I hope you will kindly take your leave."

Alexander, his face contorted in anger, stared absently at the host. He glared at Gertie, muttered 'whore' once more, and brushed passed the onlookers.

Phineas renewed his struggles as he saw his target leaving. He himself was pulled around the corner. Robert followed.

"You are in no state to confront him," Lord Dunnesford said, barely able to hold off Phineas despite his strength. With all his effort, he thrust Phineas against the wall. "You would likely kill Alexander if you touched him."

"Then I would die a happy man!"

"How will that help Gertie?"

Phineas ceased his attempts to cuff the Marquess of Dunnesford.

"I must see that she is well," he said.

But the Marquess pushed him back against the wall. "My wife is with her now. She will see that she comes to no harm."

"Gertie is with child—"

"I know. She will come home with us tonight. We will send for a doctor to see her."

"Look here, I know your wife to be friends with Gertie, but you, sir, have no place in this affair."

"I am doing what Gertie would have wanted—keeping you safe."

Phineas threw aside Dunnesford's arm. "I have no need for a protector."

"Do not render her sacrifice useless by endangering yourself."

Phineas, intending to walk away, paused. "Alexander is a bloody little cretin. I could dispense of him easily."

"No doubt. And then what? Will you live in exile? Will you ask Gertie and the babe to join you? Is that the life you wish for her?"

"Phineas," Robert pleaded, "do heed what Lord Dunnesford is saying."

"And what life would she have with Alexander?" Phineas returned. "She will be safe when I have done with him."

"If you would reconsider your situation in the light of day," Lord Dunnesford proposed, "I promise you all in my power to assist you and Gertie. I speak not because I bear you any friendship—I had advised Gertie against you—but for her sake, my wife and I would undertake much to see her happy."

As would I, Phineas thought to himself. He looked over the Marquess. The man seemed earnest, his rationale sound, but could he be trusted?

"I wish to know that Gertie is unharmed," he said, still fighting back his desire to pummel Alexander into the ground. He would have risked exile for the opportunity to bludgeon the man.

"I will have word sent to you immediately," Dunnesford assured.

Straightening himself, Phineas adjusted his coat and replied, "Very well."

Robert let out an audible sigh.

"Go home," the Marquess advised.

When they walked past the entry to the card room, the crowd had already disbursed. Neither Gertie nor Alexander remained.

Phineas allowed Robert to escort him home, but only because the latter knew better than to speak to him. Back in his apartment, Phineas allowed his valet to remove his coat and cravat, then waved the man off. He needed space and solitude to think.

She loved him.

He would have dwelled on that alone if he were not painfully aware of the difficulty she had placed herself in her attempt to save him. Once more Fate showed her ironic hand. The revelation that Gertie loved him should have brought naught but euphoria. Instead, it would bring about the very end that she had tried so hard to avoid.

"Your lordship, a woman is here to see you," Gibbons announced.

"Send her away," Phineas replied, unbuttoning his waistcoat and loosening his shirt to take a deep and full breath.

Gibbons nodded and left. Phineas poured himself a drink and sat down before the writing table. What was to be done now for Gertie?

Gibbons returned. "Pardon, your lordship, but she insists upon seeing you."

Phineas frowned. He was in no mood for the Phillipa Summers and Sarah Farringtons of the world. He doubted he had even the patience for Lady Dunnesford.

"Send her away," he repeated.

"But Lady Lowry said—"

"Lady Lowry!"

Phineas leaped from his chair and nearly knocked Gibbons over in his haste. He descended the stairs and did not slow until he saw her form in the vestibule. She was in full dress still. Upon seeing him, she threw back the hood of her ermine lined cloak. He hurried to her. The first thing he noted was the bluish mark upon her cheekbone, and suddenly he wished that he had not allowed the Marquess to dissuade him from giving Alexander a sound thrashing.

"Gertie."

She flew into his arms. He embraced her close to his bosom, soaking in the feel of her safely in his arms. The moment melted away all the agony and the suffering of the past month.

She lifted her face and again he saw the bruise. "Phineas, I have been a fool—"

He cupped her face and kissed her. She had already said all that he had ever hoped to hear. The consequences of the evening could wait. For now he wanted only to revel in her presence and demonstrate the depth of his affection by exalting her body.

His longing matched by her own, she returned his kiss fervently. They devoured one another, their passions revealed by tender lips and ardent tongue. He tasted of her long and deep for his hunger for her had been made profound by the absence. She took in his mouth as if she needed the air from his lungs. The yearning in his groin raged in response. There was no honey sweeter, no wine more intoxicating, no Bedlam more maddening than the feel of her pressing against him.

Her lips were pink and swollen when at last he pulled away from her. He swept her and the heavy silk brocade of her gown into his arms and ascended the stairs. Once in his chambers, he untied her cloak. Not able to part long from the taste of her, he crushed his lips once more to hers, determined that she should feel every ounce of the passion he felt for her.

"Gertie, the days might as well have been years," he murmured against her mouth.

"Had I but realized earlier…"she murmured in between his kisses. "Phineas, how I have missed you!"

"The past is gone. What matters is that you are where you belong."

"Yes! I belong with you. Take me, Phineas!"

His desire swelled, but he hesitated. "But are you well? Did he hurt you much?"

"It surprised me more than it hurt. I am well. Only pray do not keep me waiting!"

She began to pull out the pins in her gown. He licked his bottom lip and assisted her with undressing the bodice of her gown. When she had shed her skirt and petticoats, he caught the swell of her belly beneath her corset. Seeing the direction of his gaze, she placed a hand there.

"The knowledge that you were the one that fathered the babe has provided me the only source of brightness these past days."

He cupped her face once more. "How is it you have grown in beauty since last I saw you?"

She sidled closer to him, grinning. "Lord Barclay, if you think that flattery will aid you in your seduction, you are gravely mistaken. For I am, before now, yours to take and ravish."

Groaning, he smothered her with wet, heavy kisses. He trailed his mouth down her neck, taking mouthfuls of her smooth, taut skin. The pressure in his groin built with every whiff of her scent, every touch of her body. Pushing the chemise down past her shoulders, he showered kisses upon the skin laid bare. He had to remind himself not too grope her too roughly as she was with child, but it was no easy task to contain his ardor. He had been without her for far too long, a drought made all the more agonizing by the belief that he would never again possess her. He turned her around and began to unlace her corset, a task that forced him to slow that part of him that wanted only to throw up her chemise and allow his passions to rule his body.

"You've no need to unlace me, Phineas."

"I would see your glorious body, my love," he replied.

"I do not think I will take such care with *your* clothes," she said impishly.

The corset fell to the floor, followed by the chemise. She stood only in her garters, stocking, and shoes. His gaze perused every inch of her nakedness. Even her distended belly looked seductive, and his erection throbbed in appreciation. He put his hand gently upon her abdomen. He had never had much of an interest in procreation before, but—and his shaft was willing—he would have made a hundred babes with Gertie. She smiled up at him and he felt a blissful warmth flooding his chest.

She stepped towards him and rubbed herself against his crotch. He growled low in his throat and reached a hand to cup the bottom of a buttock. His hand closed about the flesh, remembering how her arse had quivered beneath his spanks. She pulled his waistcoat down over his arms and pressed her succulent mouth to the base of his throat. His ardor reared itself against the constraining fabric of his breeches. With his waistcoat pinning his arms to his sides, his hands could not roam about her body freely. He was content to have her take the lead, knowing he would have his moment shortly.

Pushing aside his linen, her mouth found a nipple. She sucked upon it greedily. As she sank to her knees, she slid her mouth down his front and traced the bulge of his length with her tongue. She undid his breeches. His rod sprang forth and grazed her cheek. She wrapped her hands about the shaft and covered the head with her mouth. Moaning, her eyes closed as if she had just tasted the most exquisite of desserts, she licked and lapped at him, rolling her tongue all about his erection, sucking him until his seed threatened to burst forth.

He pulled her to her feet and over to a chair. Sitting first, he positioned her above his lap and eased her down onto him. The warm wetness encasing his shaft was beyond marvelous. Reaching his arm around her hip, he fondled her clitoris. She leaned against his chest as he began to thrust his pelvis deeper into her. He turned her face back towards him so that they could join lips. She moaned against his mouth and writhed into his hand. With his other hand, he grasped a breast, brushed his thumb across the extended nipple, and kneaded the heavy flesh.

Her moaning turned into delicious grunts and gasps as she approached her climax. She trembled against him. Her cunnie clutched at him. And then the pressure building within her shattered, sending ripples of delight throughout her. She cried out. He held her tight so that she would not fall off of him. He wanted to absorb every tremor of her ecstasy. Gradually, she became heavy against him. He eased his caresses.

When her breath had settled, she turned to him. "Come, I wish for us to make love until the dawn."

Rising, she pulled him towards his bed. He kicked off the remainder of his clothing. She pushed him down into the pillows and straddled him. Her cunnie was soaking with desire and she slid easily onto him. A soft glisten of perspiration glowed upon her skin. A lovelier vision could not be had than that of his love, naked, riding him. She ground her groin against his. He assisted by thrusting his hips up at her, making her breasts bounce. He paced himself for he wanted them to spend together. Holding her hips, he eased her up and down his shaft until she was once more panting and groaning. He quickened his thrusts until he was slapping at her with a speed that made her teeth chatter. Her cunnie clenched, and her body went into a paroxysm. His desire exploded inside of her with a force that made him buck unintentionally hard against her. The sensation shot down his legs, jerking his limbs uncontrollably. He pumped himself against her, squeezing every last drop of seed into her heat. She held herself upright until the last of his tremors had been drawn, then she collapsed on top of him.

* * * * *

"I would go with you anywhere, Phineas," she murmured as she lay curled in his arms. "I know now that I could not be apart from you again. If you should go into exile, I would follow."

"That is no life for a woman with child," he said as he kissed her forehead.

"I want no life that you are not in. 'So dear I love him that with him, all deaths I could endure. Without him, live no life.'"

Her last words were barely audible as she slipped into sleep. He watched as she slept, her even breathing casting a calm upon him save for the churning of his mind. He spent more of the night watching her sleep and contemplating what they were to do now that Gertie had exposed their affair. She could not return to Alexander. Some husbands could endure being made a cuckold, but Phineas did not trust Alexander. He would not have Gertie placing herself or her unborn child in harm. But what life could they and the child have? She might profess her willingness to be with him now, but would she come to resent the bleak future their child would face?

When the first rays of morning filtered through the window, Phineas disengaged himself from Gertie and returned the circulation into his arm. He dressed in the anteroom and went to leave a note beside her in bed, wanting to kiss her but not wishing to wake her.

Dearest Gertie,

I have requested that breakfast be served to you in bed and sent word to Lady Dunnesford to bring you such items as you may need for your toilette. My servants are yours to command. I regret that I could not be present upon your waking to greet you with a kiss, but know that I am forever, with adoration and devotion, yours.

Phineas

He startled his servants with the hour and set off for Barclay House to find his brother. He was told by the butler there that his lordship was still in bed.

"But Robert always rises with the sun," Phineas contemplated.

His impatience triumphed and he made his way upstairs into the Baron's chambers. Robert lay in his bed, a compress upon his forehead.

"You have aged me ten years in a night, Phineas," Robert mumbled as he lay motionless with eyes closed.

Phineas sat down on chair near the bed. "I can hardly believe myself that foolish major wished to call me out when I had done nothing with his silly wife."

Robert propped himself up with one elbow to stare at Phineas. "Then why in bloody hell did you agree to a duel with that man?"

"Why not? I could see the man was determined. If not he, then it would have been some other affronted husband."

Groaning, Robert fell back down. "You will have your chance yet, no doubt, with the Earl of Lowry."

"Not if he can be persuaded to give up Gertie."

"You wish him to cede you his honor and his wife? My dear fellow, you have gone mad. I wash my hands of you, Phineas.

Bettina was right. You will be the death of me."

"What if I resume the barony?"

Robert raised himself again. "Eh?"

"What sort of advance do you think we could secure on the copper?"

"Ten thousand, easily. Why?"

"I wish to buy Gertie from Alexander."

Robert only frowned. "That sort of thing happens only with the lower classes. Even were Alexander willing to part with Gertie, he would simply sue you for damages."

"Alexander would be willing to part with his mother for the right price. He bears no affection for Gertie now that her funds are gone. As for *crim con*, I will not have Gertie endure such a thing. I will simply offer Alexander more than he is likely to be awarded in a *crim con* suit."

"But all the work for the copper…"

"She is worth more to me than all the copper in the world," Phineas said quietly.

"And you would take back the barony?"

"Yes. I will ask the Marquess of Dunnesford to submit before Parliament a petition for divorce. Once Gertie is free, she and I will be married. But all this must happen before the child is born."

"That is no small order."

"Love has never come easily to me."

Removing his compress, Robert sat up and faced his brother. "Is the child yours?"

"Gertie is certain, but it matters not. I will raise the child as mine own."

"What if Alexander wishes to claim the child?"

"When he discovers the child to be mine, he will want nothing to do with it. He would sooner die than see Lowry go to a child of Barclay blood."

Robert was silent in thought. "What of your trip to Scotland with Prudence?"

"I will discuss the matter with her. Regardless, I have every intention of overseeing her education and maturation henceforth."

"My God, what have you done with my brother?"

Phineas grinned. He rose to his feet. "I can depend upon your support then? I have a very important appointment with my tailor to keep."

Robert half-smiled. "Yes, yes. Be off with you then—your lordship."

CHAPTER TWENTY

GERTIE PACED THE commons near Dunnesford House. Harrietta was nursing her son, and Gertie had no wish to intrude her anxiety upon such a peaceful pair. The cool autumn wind blew all around her, but the fresh air helped to calm her nerves. She could not be sure if the strange fluttering sensations in her belly had to do with her disquiet or the life growing inside of her. She could not refrain her mind from imagining all possible outcomes of the meeting between Alexander and Vale.

"You can have the wanton harlot for all I care," she envisioned Alexander saying.

And then she would see Alexander rejecting the deal simply to spite his wife and Phineas. Gertie clasped and unclasped her hands several times. The amount Phineas was offering was a grand sum for Lowry, but perhaps Alexander would be satisfied with the income Sarah's matrimony could produce? However Alexander decided, at the least, she knew her heart, and there was comfort in that. She would be with Phineas regardless.

A man on horseback approached. Phineas!

She picked up her skirts and ran towards him. He quickly dismounted and caught her in his arms.

"Darling, you ought not run in such fashion," he said after he had nestled a kiss in her neck.

"I may be with child, but I am not incapacitated," she informed him. She searched his face for indications.

His handsome face broke into a broad smile. "You are to be mine, Gertie."

She threw her arms about his neck and held him tight. "Truly?"

"Dunnesford told me that Alexander agreed to all the terms."

"And the child?"

"Alexander has no interest in our child."

She shuddered in relief. "I have made myself sick with worry."

"As did I. I rode my poor horse around Berkeley Square what seemed a hundred times, waiting for Dunnesford to emerge. I wanted so often to enter Lowry House to confront Alexander myself, but your suggestion to have Dunnesford represent us was a wise one."

He picked her up and spun her about. She laughed, awkwardly for she could hardly believe that she was to be free, free to be with Phineas.

"Dunnesford told me that he would submit the petition for divorce tomorrow," Phineas continued, "and then you will be completely mine, my love."

"How fortunate we were that such a grand lode of copper had been discovered!"

"Even had we not that resource, dearest Gertie, I would have found a means. I would have sold my soul to possess you."

She looked into his eyes and felt her love for him swelling to such an extent that she wondered her bosom would not burst.

"You will come live with me at Barclay," he declared. "I do not think I can wait for us to be married."

"Vale and Harrietta said that I can stay at Dunnesford House for as long as I wish. It is perhaps more proper."

"Hang propriety," he growled. "It is known that we are lovers."

"Nonetheless, I do not wish for us to appear blatant or impudent before Parliament has approved our petition. Absence will make our hearts fonder."

He frowned. "You would torment me, Gertie?"

"For our future, I am willing to bear some torture today."

He thought for a moment. "I agree to this plan of yours on one condition."

She raised a brow.

"That you agree to an assignation with me at *Madame Botreaux's Ballroom of Pleasures.*"

She started. "No. That is unnecessary. I could simply visit you at your apartment as your servants have proved to be most discreet."

"I prefer *Madame Botreaux's.*"

She stepped away from him and his searching eyes. "How do you know of *Madame Botreaux's?*"

"How do you?"

"I—I heard of it from…"

She could not reveal her friends.

"The Marquess and Marchioness," he provided.

"You knew?" she gasped.

"I was told that Dunnesford was quite the deity there."

Too many thoughts were swirling in her head. How would Phineas react if he knew she had already been a patron of Madame Botreaux's? If she agreed to go with him to the *Ballroom*, she might be recognized as Lady Athena. Would Penelope then reveal her?

"You have been to *Madame Botreaux's* before?" she ventured, hoping to keep the attention upon him.

"Quite frequently."

She had her back to him and tugged at her fingers. "In the past?"

"Earlier this year."

Her voice nearly cracked. "Indeed?"

"I was quite taken by someone there."

A rage of jealousy swept through her, and she had to remind herself that his past would likely produce many opportunities for jealousy. Such ugly feelings were not productive.

"An impervious woman," he added, "but I was intent upon pursuing her. I intended to show her the error of her ways."

She wondered which of the many beautiful women at the *Ballroom* he was referring to. He stood close enough to her that his chest grazed her back. The wind blew his cloak around her. He cupped her chin and tilted her ear to his mouth.

"Lady Athena."

Her heart leaped from her. But Lady Athena was her! Should she reveal the truth to him? He was the man she loved, a man who would become her husband. She could keep no secret from him.

But how had he come across Lady Athena?

She whirled around to face him, the blood draining from her. "Hephaestus!"

"My lady," he greeted with a grin.

"How could I not have...?" she gasped, appalled at her own blindness as the visions of the *Ballroom* flashed before her and the memory of how she had responded to him surged in her body. "How long have *you* known?"

"Since the Four Horse Posting Inn."

"But you said nothing!"

"I believed if you wished me to know, you would have told me."

She glanced away from him, feeling somewhat angry that he had known all this time when she had not.

He wrapped a hand about her waist and pulled her to him. The sparkle of amusement danced in his eyes. "Do not be offended, my love. I will let you exact your vengeance upon me at *Madame Botreaux's.*"

She pursed her lips. "It will be a vengeance like you have never experienced, Hephaestus."

He grinned. "I welcome everything you would do to me, and then I will have my triumph. I am quite confident that Lady Athena will be surrendering to the greatest of bodily pleasures."

Gertie felt her knees weaken at the prospect. "You may find Lady Athena more formidable than the Countess of Lowry, sir."

He drew her even closer until she felt the hardness of his desire against her. "Make no mistake. I will achieve my conquest."

She would not have disputed him even had his mouth not claimed hers before she could utter another word. Lady Athena had long succumbed, for Phineas Barclay had conquered Lady Athena the moment he had conquered the heart of the Countess.

THE END

Other Titles by Georgette Brown

Printed in Great Britain
by Amazon

40646025R00116